"I'm not sure what _____ this story, but what I read wasn't it—this book far surpassed my expectations. Professional, well-written, well-plotted: it's an independently-published book that reads just like a traditionally-published contemporary romance."
—Erika Mathews, author of *Promise's Prayer*

"*Live Without You* is a sweet story that touches on subjects we all can relate to. In a simple yet heartfelt tone, the author weaves a story about heartache, loss, and the power of love to overcome. The love and light of Christ shine through this little book in a deep and meaningful way. The focus on first responders is also unique and made me appreciate it all the more. Highly recommended."
—Jesseca Wheaton, author of the *Questions of War* series

"Powerful, emotional, raw, and beautiful all at once. Sarah Grace truly has a talent for creating relatable characters who are just as flawed as we are, yet so amazing that we feel inspired. I loved every second of reading [*Live Without You*]."
—Ivie Brooks, author of the upcoming *Uprising Trilogy*

"Adorable, tear-jerking, and heartfelt! *Live Without You* is the best kind of story—one that the reader can slip into and experience the characters' struggles and heartache

Live Without You

To Catherine,
May you know how wild
your Heavenly Father's love
for you is! Blessings,
Sarah Grace Grzy

A NOVELLA BY

SARAH GRACE GRZY

Live Without You

A novella by Sarah Grace Grzy

Paperback ISBN: 9781793924087

Cover by Estetico Designs www.esteticodesigns.com
Interior Formatting by Victoria Lynn Designs
www.victorialynndesigns.com
Copy Edit by Bridget Marshall

Scripture taken from the New King James Version. Copyright © 1982 by Thomas Nelson, Inc. Used by permission. All rights reserved.

Printed in the USA

To the ones who feel unworthy:
May you know the Father's great love for you.
1 John 4:10

1

Multicolored Christmas lights surrounded the outdoor skating rink, yet to be taken down after the holiday season. People of all shapes and sizes filled the rink and overflowed out into the immediate area, laughing and chatting in couples and groups. An early January chill was in the air, but a sense of peace and merriment pervaded it nonetheless.

Seated on one of the numerous benches placed around the rink, Piper Redding took in the sight before her, a red plaid scarf pulled up around her neck and cheeks. She came to the rink alone, not to skate—she didn't know how—but to watch. It was her favorite place to come and relax, especially on a Friday night when the crowd was larger and she could blend in and observe.

There was something calming about people-watching on nights like tonight. There were few harsh words and laughter was frequently heard. It was a happy place, a place of community and relationship; things Piper rarely experienced. That was fine. She was a loner. And she liked it that way.

She watched as a young towheaded boy grabbed a little girl's hand and pulled her across the ice. Piper smiled bittersweetly, pain tightening her chest as she thought of her brother trying to teach her six-year-old self to skate—with little success. After the ice had broken and he'd fallen in up to his waist, she'd had no desire to try the experiment again, regardless of the fact that the ice refroze and her brother had not been injured. She leaned her head back against the bench and closed her eyes, letting her ears absorb the happy sounds around her as she tried to tune out her memories.

So few of them were worth reliving.

Just as she was considering heading home, a sharp, familiar, and dreaded sound echoed into the night, shattering the peaceful atmosphere.

A gunshot.

Piper's heart rate kicked into double-time. She suddenly found it hard to breathe as she scrambled to her feet, feeling stuck in slow-motion. Her mind flashed to a dark Chicago alley, but she tried to push the memory away. This was one she never wanted to remember.

Oh God, please no, her mind begged, forgetting that she'd decided praying was a waste of time.

There was complete silence for a few brief heartbeats of time before more shots rang out and people screamed and surged in an attempt at self-preservation. But she couldn't move. Her brain felt short-circuited. She was frozen. Numb. Until a blazing pain seared through her shoulder. Stumbling to her knees as her eyes glazed over, she clutched a hand to the pain as if to make it stop.

Surely, she was dreaming this. She pulled her hand away and squinted at it.

Blood. So much blood.

Was it her blood? Or was it Paul's?

It was hers. This was it then. She was going to die, as she should have six years ago.

If only he could have been spared.

Conscious thought left her as the sights and sounds of the pandemonium around her faded into black nothingness.

Exiting his car and tucking his hands in his back pockets, Ezra Bryant strolled aimlessly across the park. It was the perfect day for a walk. Most people would say it was too cold, but he didn't care. Northern Washington wasn't for wimps, and those who didn't like the weather . . . well, they could move to Phoenix.

A blast of wind pushed at his back and he shivered. Maybe it was a bit cold once the sun started to go down. . . .

He took a deep breath and exhaled, wishing he could rid himself of the trauma of the day as easily. Someone had died. That was always depressing. A patient flatlining before even making it onto the ambulance gurney was something every paramedic dreaded, he more than others. It dredged up too many reminders of the past. He had continued resuscitation procedures the entire six-minute drive to the hospital, and the ER staff picked up where he left off. But he had known . . . It was too late.

The sound of firecrackers and screams rent the air from the east side of the park, startling him. Eight days into the new year and people were still reveling, but today he felt anything but celebratory.

Then his heart stuttered as realization dawned. Lord, have mercy.

Those weren't firecrackers.

Ezra pulled his radio from his belt as he set off at a run back towards his car to grab his medic bag, prayers flying heavenward even as he radioed in the call.

By the time he reached the ice rink, red and blue lights filled the area and sirens had replaced the sounds of gunshots. He pushed his way towards an officer to proffer his help, scanning the area for injured victims as he went. With as many shots as he had heard, there was no way there weren't a few casualties.

Then he saw her.

She lay crumpled on her side on the ground, facing away from him, red-brown hair and blood intermixing across the cold pavement.

Ezra dropped to his knees beside her and pulled a pair of latex gloves on, his mind already laser-focused on his job. He quickly scanned the woman for further injuries before bracing her and gently rolling her onto her back. Heavy bleeding from the left clavicle, no spurting, and a steady, if labored, rise and fall of her chest. He pulled a large dressing out of his bag, packing the wound with it and applying pressure with the heel of his hand to slow the profuse bleeding. He put his fingertips against her neck. Her pulse was slow, weak, and erratic, her breathing shallow, and skin pale and clammy. No exit wound, and it didn't look like the bullet hit either lung or heart. Lucky woman. Blessed. Glancing back at her face, he noticed her eyes had opened and stared unfocused into the distance beyond his head.

He started. Why did she look familiar?

"Ma'am, ma'am, can you hear me? My name is Ezra. I'm a paramedic. I'm going to help you. Just try to stay with me, all right? Can you tell me your name?"

He was stalling for time. Another few minutes and she wasn't going to make it. Keeping one hand still pressing against her wound, he was reaching for his radio to get an ambulance ETA when she spoke.

"Pi-per . . . help . . ." Her voice was barely a whisper, and he read her lips more than heard her voice.

She was in shock, her body rapidly shutting down from blood loss and pain. With his free hand he grabbed an emergency blanket and tucked it around her, then returned that hand to her neck to monitor her pulse.

"All right, Piper. The ambulance is almost here," he assured.

Piper . . . her name sounded familiar, too, but he still couldn't place it.

The emergency vehicle screamed to a stop behind him and two EMTs unloaded a gurney. One of them, a co-worker, Aimee, stopped on the other side of him.

"Ez? What are you doing here? Thought you were off shift." Her quick eyes were already assessing their patient as she spoke.

"I was, but I was in the area and stopped to help." He hurriedly filled her in on what he knew as they worked to get the woman stabilized and in the ambulance.

As Ezra climbed up into the vehicle after Aimee, pulling the door shut behind him, it hit him like a lightning bolt.

Piper Redding. Paul Redding's kid sister. He turned to look at her. Although she wasn't much of a kid anymore. Nine years had changed her a lot—that much he could tell even with an oxygen mask obscuring half her face.

The question was—what was she doing in Washington, halfway across the country from her Chicago home? And what about Paul?

Live Without You

Piper attempted to open her eyes, but they felt glued shut. She finally pried them open, and the room around her blurred and spun, slowly coming into focus. Everything in her narrow line of vision was white. Where was she? Why couldn't she remember anything? Why did nothing make sense? Her brain didn't seem able to function beyond asking answerless questions.

She tried to sit up, but at the movement, pain roared through her left shoulder, causing her head to spin in wild circles and making it hard to breathe. A groan seeped through her clenched teeth as she gingerly laid her head back against the pillow. She could take stock of the situation from a prone position then.

Or not. Every heartbeat pulsed pain through her head, her neck, her shoulder. And her brain still felt dead. Sucking in a slow, deep breath as she slowly drifted off, she decided everything could wait until later. . . .

When she awoke again, the room was dim. Piper decided not to sit up this time. Making the same mistake twice was always something she tried to avoid. Instead, she let her eyes travel the room, taking in her surroundings. Various monitors and gadgets blinked and beeped softly in the darkness. An IV protruded from the back of her right hand, and some kind of probe or monitor had attached itself to her index finger. Her left arm was heavily bandaged and taped to her chest. She wracked her still-foggy brain for answers.

Then squeezed her eyes shut as it all rushed back in a flood. The screams, the pain, the rough gravel underneath her cheek.

And the looming blackness and mocking voices inside her head.

It's all your fault. If it hadn't been for you, he'd still be here. Loser. It should have been you. It's your turn, now. This is what you deserve. It's all your fault.

All your fault.

All her fault.

Breathing heavily, Piper dragged her eyelids open again. She glanced wildly around the room, as if looking for the source of the voices that sounded so clear.

Just then, the door pushed open and a woman in scrubs entered. "You're awake!" Her mellow, Africanaccented voice soothed Piper instantly. She opened her mouth, but no sound came out. The woman grabbed a cup seemingly from nowhere and held the straw to Piper's lips as she introduced herself. "My name is Cecile, and I'll be your nurse for the next shift. If there's anything at all you need, hon, you just press this lil' button and I'll come a-runnin'. All right?"

Piper nodded, and, when she tried to speak again, she found her voice did indeed still work.

"How long have I been out?" she asked.

"Well, I'd say 'bout twenty-four hours now. You woke up a few times, but we've kept you pretty heavily sedated to give your body a head start at healin'."

"When can I go home?"

Cecile chuckled. "Ain't you an eager beaver? Not yet, child. I'd say Monday, if all goes well. It's Saturday evening," she added, seeing the question in Piper's eyes.

While she was speaking, the nurse had messed with Piper's IV. She suddenly felt like weights were dragging her eyelids down and her brain was powering off.

Patting her arm, Cecile spoke again in softer tones. "You just rest now, honey. And when you wake up, the doctor will explain everything."

Piper was out again before the nurse even left the room.

◆

Monday morning, Ezra followed the dark-skinned nurse down the hospital corridor that was bustling with an unusual number of visitors and staff. The nurse chattered on as if she knew him—which she probably did—although he couldn't say he had ever officially met her before.

What was becoming known as the Shiloh Park Shooting was making national news. A psychopath with a gun wreaking havoc in small-town Washington. He'd been keeping an eye on the news and was relieved that Piper's name hadn't been released to the media as of yet. But it was only a matter of time. . . .

Finally reaching the designated door, the nurse gave it a light knock before pushing it open and entering. Ezra stayed in the doorway, a hand tucked in his jeans pocket. The nurse helped the girl in the bed to a sitting position as she spoke. "You got a special visitor today, hon."

"Who is it, Miss Cecile?" The girl's voice was soft and strained as she sat up, favoring her left shoulder. The nurse motioned him forward with an introduction.

"This young man was the one who saved your life the other day."

Ezra's face grew warm, but he stepped forward and offered his right hand. "Ezra Bryant. And I really didn't do much." He smiled and met the girl's—no, young woman's—eyes. Light red-brown hair was gathered up in a messy bun, accentuating her familiar small oval face and brown eyes that flickered with confusion. The white hospital bed seemed to dwarf her already small frame, as did the sling on her left arm.

She gave him a tentative, shy smile and shook his hand. "Piper Redding. Thank you for what you did." Her words were simple, but he could hear the sincerity behind them. She motioned to a nearby chair and he pulled it closer to the bed before taking a seat.

An awkward silence fell on the room, disturbed only by the nurse checking various machines.

Ezra cleared his throat and spoke up. "Well, at least it's not your right arm," he said with a grin, gesturing to her sling.

Piper stared at him blankly for a second before blinking.

"I'm left-handed."

The grin slid off his face. "Oh." He coughed. "I'm sorry." And . . . the awkward silence was back.

"So what do you do for a living?" Piper asked.

He paused and glanced at the nurse now exiting the room. "I'm a paramedic."

Color tinged her pale-white cheeks. "Oh. I guess that makes sense." She smiled sheepishly.

Ezra chuckled and leaned forward, resting his elbows on his knees. "You don't recognize me?"

Piper stared at him contemplatively, confusion coloring her features. After a second, she shook her head. "I'm sorry, no. Should . . . should I?" Her voice was tentative.

He shook his head as well, disappointed. "Guess not. It's been nearly nine years."

"Nine years since what? I . . . I'm sorry, my brain is still foggy from the pain medicine, the doctor says."

"Since you saw me last. I was Paul's roommate and friend. We went to school together. I guess I was surprised you didn't know me because you hung around with us so much. How is—what's wrong?" He broke off when he saw her face. As he had spoken, her face had gone even whiter—although he didn't know how that was possible—and pain flickered through her eyes, darkening until a shutter covered them.

She swallowed and shook her head, looking down at her lap now. "N-nothing. I'm fine. What were you asking?" Her voice quavered a bit in spite of her denial. He wasn't believing for one moment "nothing" was wrong.

"I was going to ask . . . how is Paul?"

Piper seemed to crumple in on herself, and Ezra panicked. What had he said? *Lord, give me wisdom. And help me not to say stupid stuff . . . for once in my life.* He scooted closer to the bed and placed a hand on her good arm. "Piper, please tell me what's wrong."

With a deep breath, a straightening of her spine, and a hardening of her eyes, she went from broken to emotionless robot in a matter of seconds; the transformation astounded him. How did she do that? She swallowed and finally spoke, looking him in the eye. "Paul died six years ago." Her tone was flat, empty.

Horror filled him—not just at her shocking revelation, but at the clumsiness of his words. He stared at her before squeezing his eyes shut and pressing his fingertips to his forehead as he processed her information. He dealt with death and loss every day as part of his job, yet it still hurt deeply each time. And this was more personal. He wanted to curl up in a ball, to scream "whys" heavenward, but he wouldn't. He couldn't. He was too late.

"I'm so, so sorry, Piper," he whispered, meeting her eyes. "I had no idea." She nodded an acknowledgment, staring off into the distance, rubbing the heel of one hand with the fingers of the other, no doubt lost in a different world, a different time. He patted her arm and she looked at him. "Please let me know if I can help you in any way." He swallowed—hard. "Anything."

Piper nodded again, this time with a faint smile. "Thank you, Ezra." She paused. "I hope this doesn't sound strange, but . . . I've missed you." She seemed to want to add more, but didn't.

Ezra wanted to ask so desperately how Paul had died. But he wouldn't. Piper obviously still needed some distance from the subject, and he would do some checking around later.

He cleared his throat and tried to find a new topic. "So. When did you move to the gorgeous state of Washington?" He sat back in his chair and kept his tone purposefully light. Piper relaxed against the pillows behind her back, clearly glad for the change of subject.

"Only a few months ago. I'd been wanting to leave Chicago for a while, and the timing was right and my job allowed it, so . . . I did."

"What's your job?"

"I'm a freelance web developer and graphic designer."

He raised his eyebrows, impressed. "Wow. That's awesome."

They chatted for another fifteen minutes on trivial matters, such as coffee—she hated it, he couldn't live without it—and so on, the ease between them growing. Years couldn't completely disintegrate a long-time friendship.

"So when and how are you going home? You can't drive." He gestured to her arm. "Do you have someone to take you?"

"Today, finally. Cecile said she'd get the discharge papers ready. And I . . . guess I hadn't thought much about the second part of your question. Figured I'd call a taxi. I don't know anyone here yet." The thought seemed to pain her.

Ezra raised his eyebrows and sought to keep the smirk off his face. "This isn't the big city, y'know. We don't have taxis. An Uber, maybe, if you're lucky." He winked. "And you know me."

Piper's face fell. "Oh. I guess I didn't think of that . . ."

He couldn't help himself and started laughing. "I guess you haven't been here long, have you? I'll take you home," he said as if the matter was decided.

Surprise widened her eyes. "Oh no, I can't ask you to do that! I'll figure something out," she protested.

"Got news for you, Miss Redding, you didn't ask— I offered." He gave an elaborate bow. "Taxi driver at your service."

She giggled and bit her lip, thinking. "All right, fine. But you have to promise to take some Christmas cookies off my hands. I made way too many last week."

Ezra straightened. "Hey, I'll do almost anything for cookies. You've got a deal." He put out his hand and gave hers a playful shake.

Live Without You

3

Two police officers showed up to speak with her before she was discharged from the hospital. Somehow, Ezra's silent presence was comforting as she answered their intimidating questions. Finally, after the officers left, after paperwork and lectures from her doctor, and more lectures and hugs from Cecile, Piper was free.

She followed Ezra out of the hospital into the snow-covered parking lot, having refused the offered wheelchair. Her purse was draped over her right shoulder and the duffel bag the hospital had given her for her belongings was in Ezra's hands.

Tilting her face towards the sunlight while she walked, she breathed deeply of the pine-scented air. She was so ready to be home. A wave of dizziness washed over her, and she paused and took a deep breath, waiting for it to pass. Her doctor had said that would be normal for the first few weeks because of the blood loss. She glanced up to see Ezra standing at her shoulder, watching her intently.

"Dizzy?" he asked.

She nodded and took another breath, then winced as it stabbed pain through her shoulder. Why did everything have to hurt? Piper started walking again, and Ezra just silently took her arm, allowing her to lean on him for the rest of the short walk to his car.

He stopped beside an olive-colored Subaru Impreza and clicked the unlock button on the fob. "This is it." He tossed her duffel into the back seat and opened the passenger side door for her.

She smiled up at him before climbing in the car. He wasn't your cliché "tall, dark, and handsome," but there was a compelling sincerity in his square face and green eyes, and his brown hair glinted in the sunlight.

She buckled the seat belt over herself while taking note of the cleanliness of the car. For a guy's car, it was surprisingly clean, and while definitely not new, it was clear the owner took good care of it.

"Nice car," she said as Ezra seated himself in the driver's seat and started the ignition.

He grinned at her and petted the dash. "Thanks. She's my baby. So where are we going?" He glanced over his shoulder as he backed out of the parking space and pulled out of the lot.

Piper hid a grimace at the twinge in her shoulder as he went over a small bump. The pain meds the doctor had given her worked well—unless something bumped her or she moved her arm. "I live on Taylor Street, just off of Fir Avenue. Do you know that area?"

He squinted in thought. "Mm, yep, I think so. Here—" He pulled his phone out of the cupholder and handed it to her. "Plug your address in on the GPS app. That'll be easiest." She did so, and set the phone back on the dash when she finished.

A peaceful silence descended on the car as she watched the scenery blur past. She'd only been in this part of town once or twice since moving, so the area was mostly unfamiliar. Within minutes the quiet whir of the car was slowly lulling her. Her shoulder was starting to throb, too, and she couldn't wait to curl up on the comfy couch in her living room. She leaned her head back against the headrest and out of the corner of her eye saw Ezra glancing her way every so often. "What's wrong?" she finally asked.

"Are you doing okay?" He seemed concerned.

"Mmhm. Just tired. Thanks for asking." Piper leaned her head back again and closed her eyes.

"You know, you should take it easy for the next few weeks. Gunshot wounds are not something to be messed with. And if you feel any—"

Piper raised a hand and cut him off. "Ezra, please. I've heard that same lecture twice already."

He chuckled sheepishly. "Sorry. It's the medic in me . . ."

Piper flashed him a brief grin. "Trust me, I know. I lived with one . . ." Her voice caught and she swallowed, turning her gaze out the window and away from the man whose mere presence was dredging up so many memories she had tried to forget.

There was silence again for a few moments before Ezra spoke softly. "Want to talk about it?"

She didn't have to think twice about her answer. "No." No, she didn't want to talk about it. No, she didn't want to think about it, remember it. And yes . . . she wanted to erase the event from history.

Ezra chewed on the inside of his cheek and gripped the wheel tighter, glancing again at Piper out of the corner of his eye. Even six years later, it was clear this woman still wrestled with her brother's death. He didn't even know how his friend had died, but he wanted to help her. The gotta-fix-it part of him screamed at him to do something, fix it, make it better. However he'd died, Paul wouldn't have wanted his baby sister to live like this. Paul had doted on his only sibling.

He would help her—in any way he could.

22

For Paul's sake.

Ezra turned the corner and pulled into the driveway the GPS called out as Piper's. The house was small— only a few hundred square feet, he'd guess. Square, painted white with blue trim work and Christmas lights everywhere, it looked distinctly Piper-like. Classy. Her dark gray Accord sat in the driveway, courtesy of the Arlington police department, he knew. Piper sat up and reached to unbuckle herself, then sucked in a breath in pain. Ezra reached over and unclicked her belt before resting a hand on her knee. She looked so pale.

"Hey. You okay?"

On a slow exhale, she said, "I will be. Apparently, I need to find those painkillers the doctor gave me sooner rather than later." She pushed her door open and carefully slid out, and he did the same, grabbing her duffel and a cardboard box from the back seat. He followed her up the walkway through the few inches of snow that had accumulated over the weekend and watched while she unlocked the front door. She motioned him to enter ahead of her, then frowned when she noted the box in his arms.

"What's in the box?"

"Food. The ladies at my church compiled some things for the victims of the shooting." As he talked, he stepped into her entryway and slipped his wet boots off. Looking behind him, he saw that she still stood outside the door, staring at him. He raised his eyebrows at her questioningly.

"But . . . but . . ." She finally stepped in and shut the door. "Why? They don't know me."

He shrugged. "They don't have to. They just wanted to help."

She smiled gratefully. "Thank them for me."

Ezra nodded, glancing at his surroundings as she led him further into the house. "Nice place."

"Thanks. It's taken a bit, but it's finally starting to feel like home."

The entryway let into the open main area, with the dining room and kitchen beyond it. The walls were mainly white, with blue and blue-gray accents and a homey wood trim throughout. Eclectic but peaceful-looking decor was everywhere, yet somehow the house still maintained an uncluttered atmosphere. Christmas lights were strung anywhere possible—as they always were at Paul's home in Chicago every Christmas time he could remember. Piper had always loved Christmas lights. One area that caught his attention was the front corner of the living room. A desk sat there, buried underneath a myriad of technology: three monitors with several cords snaking across and under the desk, two keyboards, and various other unidentifiable objects. He never was much for tech, but it was clear Piper was.

Ezra turned to watch as Piper unzipped her coat and awkwardly tried to pull it off without the use of her injured arm that was still in a sling. He stepped up behind her. "Let me." She huffed and let him gently tug it off, taking care not to bump her shoulder. She sighed in relief.

"Thanks. This is going to take some getting used to," she said, gesturing to the sling. "Do you want some hot cocoa or anything? I can't thank you enough for bringing me home."

Ezra paused, then shook his head, noting the gray edging her eyes and her pale cheeks. "No, thanks. I have to get to work—I have the evening shift—and you should take some of your pain meds and a nap."

She rolled her eyes, her tired grin belying her annoyance. "Yes, Mother . . . But really, thank you for everything." Her tone changed from sarcasm to sincerity, her brown eyes bright with gratitude. "Oh! The cookies!" She walked towards the kitchen and pulled a tin out of a cupboard.

Ezra shook his head and called after her. "I didn't do anything worth talking about, but . . . you're welcome." She came back and handed him the tin, and he took it with a smile. "Thanks. Let me know if you need anything at all. I'd be more than happy to bring you some groceries or something." He pulled a scrap of paper from his pocket on which he'd already scribbled his name and phone number and handed it to her.

Piper took it, glanced at it, and nodded. "I'll text you so you have my number."

"Great." He turned towards the door, but paused at her voice.

"Ezra?"

He looked back at her and was worried by the look on her face. "Yes?"

"Who . . . how many . . . others . . . ?"

He'd been hoping she wouldn't ask him that. "Two."

Piper just continued to look at him. Swallowing hard, he answered her unspoken question. "Dead. Both of them."

Horror, grief, and what he recognized as a deep, indescribable pain simultaneously flashed across her face for brief seconds before it disappeared behind a solid wall of stoicism. The raw intensity and subsequent transformation both shocked and scared him. Just as it had at the hospital.

"And the shooter?"

He shook his head. "The police arrested him late Friday night."

As Ezra got into his car and headed towards the department, he sent a quick prayer heavenward. "Lord, let me be a blessing to Piper. Heal her heart, Father . . . she needs your love."

He drummed the steering wheel with his thumbs. What had happened to Paul anyway? He would have been . . . Ezra quickly did the mental math. Twenty-four. Too young to die, most would say. But Ezra knew better. Everything happens for a reason. Although he of all people would know it didn't make the pain any less. . . .

Piper stepped to the window and watched Ezra stride down the driveway to his car, slide in, and drive off.

Ezra Bryant.

Of all people.

She'd left Chicago to rid herself of the constant reminders—and the guilt that came with them—of a man named Paul Redding.

Her brother. Her best friend. The only person who had actually, really, cared and been there for her. The one person who had protected her.

Then he had left too. Just like all the others. And it was her fault.

She shook her head to clear the thoughts of Paul and Ezra and swallowed down the guilt that rose like bile in her throat. Turning and taking a deep breath, she winced at the pain that shot through her shoulder and the accompanying dizziness. Where did she put the medicine the doctor had given her? She dug through the duffel bag Ezra had deposited on the couch, then dug through her purse before finally finding the small yellow bottle.

Piper popped two of the white caplets in her mouth and swallowed them with a sip of water. A nap sounded more than wonderful, but the food Ezra had brought needed to find a home first. She made short work of sorting through the box despite being one-handed. Three casseroles, a pasta dish, two mason jars of soup, and brownies. She put most of the items in the freezer, leaving out a jar of soup for her dinner.

Finished, she glanced around her house—and sighed deeply. It was a mess, as it usually was. But it was a job for another time . . . She was exhausted.

Piper dropped to the couch and tugged the fuzzy duck-egg-blue blanket hanging over the back onto her body. Fatigue—physical and mental—pulled her eyelids shut and within minutes, she was asleep.

zra unlocked his apartment door, entered, and shut it behind himself, throwing the deadbolt in place. He yawned and checked the time on the clock hanging on the far wall. 8:27 a.m. Working the graveyard shift wasn't his first choice, but since most of the other EMS workers had families, he'd opted to.

He strode to his small bedroom off the main area, dropped his bag on the bed, and changed out of his uniform. After bumping up the thermostat a few notches, he headed to the kitchen and pulled eggs and cheese out of the refrigerator, making himself a breakfast sandwich. Grabbing his antiquated laptop off the couch, he sat and took a bite of his meal as he waited for it to boot up. And waited. And waited. Maybe he should ask Piper about upgrading the old beast.

He typed in his login information and took a deep breath, opened the browser window, and typed keywords into the search engine. *Paul Redding, Chicago.*

He scrolled through the search results, finding a website for a photographer and several social media profiles. Not helpful. Adding a few more specific words, he pressed the enter key and held his breath.

Now this was more like it. He clicked the first link—an obituary for Paul Aaron Redding, age twenty-four, passed away nearly six years ago on January twenty-second. The article mentioned surviving family members, his brief career as a paramedic, etc. But nothing about how or why he had died. Ezra backtracked to the search results and scrubbed a hand across his eyes, swallowing the emotion burning in his throat. Scrolling a bit further, he found a news article dated three days after Paul's death.

Man Caught in Crosshairs of Gang Fight

"Paul A. Redding, a paramedic with the City of East Chicago Emergency Medical Services, was killed on January 22, 2011, at approximately 9:30 p.m. Redding was on foot, allegedly heading to his home when shooting broke out in a nearby alleyway. He was hit in the chest and arm by stray bullets, and was pronounced dead on arrival by emergency personnel. The shooter has been identified as a known gang member, who is now in custody of . . ."

Ezra's eyes stopped reading as his mind struggled to comprehend what he'd just read. Eyes burning, he rubbed a palm down his face as he fought to keep a hold on the grief that gripped him tightly. Paul didn't just die. He'd been murdered. How had he not known? He should have known. He and Paul had been close nearly all their lives, it felt like. But then Ezra had left. And never apologized. If only he had known. . . .

He shoved his sandwich aside, appetite now gone, and blinked away the tears clouding his vision. His heart ached. For Paul, a life so senselessly lost. For Piper, and all she'd lost. And for himself. For missed opportunities and broken friendships.

✦

A volley of gunshots poured forth from the nearby alleyway and she found herself frozen. She couldn't scream, react. She felt like she was a stone figurine—until her brother's guttural shout broke through the haze just before he tackled her, his lean, muscled body taking her painfully to the cold, wet pavement. Then there was silence. Still, empty, silence.

And blood. So much blood.

It flowed over her, causing nausea to swirl in her belly. She fought the panic clawing at her throat and rolled out from underneath the still form of her brother. She got to her knees, and looked down. Crimson soaked her sweater, her hands, and felt slick on her cheek. She looked to her brother, but he was gone. A pool of blood on the pavement was all that was left.

A scream rent the air, and she barely recognized it as coming from her own throat.

"Paul! You can't leave me!" Great shuddering sobs shook her body and red emergency lights garishly mixed with the red blood that swirled around her . . .

Piper jerked awake and sat straight up, staring wildly around her, her heartbeat racing and the throb in her shoulder matching it beat for beat. Her skin was damp and chilled, but she felt hot, and swiped a bead of sweat from her forehead.

They were back.

The nightmares had haunted—tormented—her for over a year after Paul's death, and slowly, ever so slowly, disappeared with the changing of the seasons. Disappeared for good, she thought, but apparently not. Piper wiped at the wetness rolling down her cheeks and took a deep breath, willing her heart and mind—along with the tears—to stop racing. But the tears only came faster.

Why? Hadn't she suffered enough without having to relive it?

Why, God?

As usual, there was no reply. But then, she hadn't been expecting one. There hadn't been one for years. Somewhere along the years after Paul's death, the answers stopped coming. They just faded away. At one time, God had answered her prayers, her questions.

She'd known He was there—had felt His love. But the silence had grown, as had the emptiness in her heart. First Paul left, then God Himself did, too. Leaving her alone and lonely.

She knew the "good-Christian-answers" to such thoughts: God will never leave us nor forsake us and all that. But then why did He feel so far away?

Piper angrily shoved those thoughts away and stood up off the couch. She took two steps, only to find herself falling, dizziness clutching her. Instinctively, she reached her left arm out to break her fall. Then gasped when pain flowed like an electrical current through her body as her shoulder took her weight. She whimpered and curled her arm towards her chest, rocking back and forth and letting the tears she'd shoved away earlier flow hot and fast.

The stupid sling. She'd taken it off and tossed it on the floor when she'd crashed to the couch, exhausted, and now it stabbed her in the back by tripping her. She sent it a glare. Knowing her luck, she probably ripped out her stitches. She cringed and palmed away the tears before gingerly peeking under the bandage on her shoulder. She gulped when she saw the gruesome sight for the first time. It was black and blue, and the skin was mangled and held together by black thread. It oozed a little, but it didn't look like she pulled out any stitches. Sighing in relief, she sat back on the couch and tugged the traitorous sling back over her forearm and tightened the straps around her now-throbbing shoulder.

It was definitely time again for some of those pain meds the doctor had given her. And some hot cocoa.

Yes, definitely hot cocoa.

She grabbed two of the tiny white pills from the bottle on the coffee table and downed them, then headed to the kitchen and poured milk in the little pot that sat on her stove for just such occasions. Adding a dash of vanilla extract and a pinch of salt, unsweetened cocoa powder and a tablespoon of sugar, she awkwardly stirred it with her right hand.

She knew she should have taken that dare from her brother to teach herself to be ambidextrous. The memory tugged up the corners of her lips. Before she pushed it away.

Remembering only hurt.

But all she could seem to do lately was remember— whether she liked it or not. With the recent . . . interesting events in her life, she shouldn't have been surprised. The brain worked in funny ways. First getting shot—of all things—then Paul's best friend showing up, saving her life.

Piper shook her head. The coincidences were far from amusing. She must have known in her subconscious that Ezra had moved to Washington. But for them to both end up in the same small town of Arlington in the northern end of the state? Perhaps not coincidence. Maybe it had been God leading her here . . . She snorted at the thought, then jumped as the cocoa mixture on the stove started to bubble over. She flicked the burner off and carefully poured the contents of the pot into her favorite turquoise mug.

Well, if God truly did lead her to cross paths with Ezra Bryant then it was strange that He'd been so silent on other matters.

Live Without You

5

zra grabbed the blue medic bag and jumped out of the ambulance before his partner, Tyler Collens, had even shifted into park. It was a cardiac arrest call, and there was no time for dillydallying.

Not that there ever was as a paramedic.

He jogged up the front porch steps of a small, '80s-style ranch house, and, before he could even knock, a plump, out-of-breath woman with gray hair hurriedly greeted him and led him through the house, Tyler not far behind. Reaching the living room, he found an ashen-faced man with hair that matched his wife's slumped on the couch. Ezra's adrenaline flowed and his mind spun as he rapidly assessed the situation. He checked the man's vitals and asked the woman routine questions as Tyler readied the AED machine.

No heartbeat. Ezra grunted. "Not today," he muttered as he shifted the man to lay on the floor, then ripped open the victim's shirt and started CPR while Tyler slapped on the AED pads.

"Clear," Tyler called.

Ezra leaned back and held his breath as the electricity jolted the man's body.

Stepping forward again, he checked the man's vitals. Still nothing. *No, no, no. I can't deal with this right now, Lord.*

They repeated the procedure twice more, following the machine's robotic orders, and Ezra's own heart sank as each minute passed with no signs of life. Finally, he breathed a sigh of a relief at the rewarding *thud, thud, thud* of the man's heart. Ezra and Tyler worked to transfer the man onto the stretcher and lift him into the ambulance while trying not to trip over the hovering, now-weeping wife. They worked so well together, they didn't even have to communicate their moves to the other.

Tyler Collens had been his partner for seven of the eight years Ezra had been a paramedic in Arlington, and they had quickly become close friends. Tyler had been the first to give him a true welcome after moving in, and now was practically a brother.

Nearly as close as Paul had been.

By the time they made it back to the department, their shift had ended. After collecting his duffel and other items from the locker room, Ezra pushed out the back door and struck out across the parking lot, pulling his keys out of his pocket as he went. His back muscles screamed from the tension of the day and a headache throbbed at the base of his skull. Memories he didn't want pushed themselves to the forefront of his mind. He thought he'd dealt with them years ago, but they still came back at the most unwanted times.

His mom. Pale and unresponsive on the floor. Him on his knees beside her, sweat and tears dripping off his face as he administered CPR. For ten minutes. Then fifteen. Until ambulance sirens sounded outside their house and a paramedic tugged him back. His dad knelt behind him, an arm wrapped around his shuddering shoulders as Ezra doubled over under the unutterable pain that cleaved through his heart at the knowledge that his mother's heart had stopped.

Forever.

He'd only been gone for twenty minutes. Twenty mere minutes. But it was too long, and he was too late.

He'd failed her when she needed him the most.

A car alarm blared and he jumped, startled out of his thoughts. Looking up, he found Tyler—still in his steel-gray paramedic's uniform—leaning against the side of Ezra's car, a smirk making a white gash through the blond stubble on his chin. Ezra rolled his eyes and cleared the emotion in his throat as he punched the panic button on the fob to turn off the alarm.

"Don't you have something better to do with your day than giving me a headache—literally?" Ezra tossed his things in the back of the car and gave Tyler a shove. "And don't touch my car." He walked around to the driver's side door and slid in. Ty crammed his large frame in on the opposite side with a grumble under his breath that sounded like an insult towards his car.

"Hey, talk nice about my baby." Ezra elbowed him.

Ty just rolled his eyes. "So what do you wanna do?" It seemed that Ezra was Tyler's only source of entertainment these days with how much he wanted to hang out. "Energizer Bunny Ty" also didn't sleep—ever, apparently. And if he did, Ezra wasn't sure when it was.

Ezra tapped his thumbs against the steering wheel, thinking, then cranked up the heat before answering. "Man, it's freezing today. Listen, if I let you meet someone, will you behave yourself?"

Tyler straightened in his seat and sent a wide-eyed stare to Ezra. "Dude, is it a girl?"

Ezra groaned and thumped the man on the back of the head. "Yeah, it is, but it's not like that." His dating life—or lack thereof—was under constant scrutiny of the guys at the department, and while Tyler didn't actually date either, that didn't stop him from joining in on the fun.

"C'mon man, spill it."

Ezra took a deep breath and let it out at the niggling of guilt that wormed its way through his heart. "I had a buddy back in Chicago. We went to high school together, and roomed together through college, until I . . . came here after my mom died." What he wouldn't give to change that day . . . and several other also terrible days. "Anyway, I treated his sister—whom he was really close with—the other day, and she told me her brother had died." Ezra paused and stared out the window and Tyler exhaled on a low whistle.

"Aw, I'm sorry, Ez." One of the things Ezra appreciated about Tyler was that while he could be a goofball, he also knew when to be serious.

Ezra shook his head. "It's fine." Sort of. Not really. "But anyway, she's basically housebound and doesn't know anybody here—except for some nurse." He chuckled. "So I thought she might like some company."

Tyler let out a laugh. "Nurse? You mean Cecile Tompkins?"

Ezra slanted him a look. "I think that was her name—why?"

Tyler practically hooted—his booming laugh filling the small amount of airspace in the car. "How do you not know Cecile? Everybody knows Cecile." He chuckled again and shook his head. "She's a sweet lady. A real character."

Ezra raised his brows. "O-kay then. So, you in?"

"Sure. Anybody Cecile likes is a good egg." He laughed again. Ezra just shook his head and pulled out his phone to text Piper with the offer of company and pizza. Her response came within minutes.

Aw, you don't have to do that! But I've made it a rule to never turn down free pizza . . . ;)

Ezra chuckled and sent a reply as Tyler continued to amuse himself cracking jokes.

Hey, that sounds like a rule I can get behind. Be there in a bit.

He dropped his phone in the cup holder and turned up the volume on the radio, sending Tyler a pointed look to get him to shut up. "I told you to behave."

"Yeah man, I will . . . when we get there. By the way," Tyler pointed an accusatory finger Ezra's direction. "Why are you so uptight lately?"

Ezra sent him a glare before merging into the mid-morning traffic. "I'm not uptight."

"Yeah, you are. You about hyperventilated when that guy's heart wouldn't start this morning."

Ezra frowned, keeping his eyes on the road. "I did not."

"You did." Tyler paused, then his tone softened in understanding. "You gotta leave the past in the past, Ez. It's where it belongs."

"What are you, my shrink now?" he growled.

His bitter comment had Ty sending him a whipped-puppy-dog look. Funny how such a big, rough-and-tumble-looking guy could so effectively pull off that particular look. His poor parents.

Ezra sighed, his frustration draining. "I'm sorry, Ty."

Tyler nodded. "We're good. But you still need to lighten up."

"I'd really lighten up if you pay for the pizza."

"What? No way, dude!" Tyler protested. "It's your date!"

Ezra groaned and slapped a hand against the wheel instead of Tyler's head. "It's not a date!"

Tyler just cackled gleefully.

Piper one-handedly sent her text reply to Ezra and sat back down with a groan.

No, no, no. This was a bad idea. Why didn't she think this through? She didn't need more people in her life. Actually, she didn't have any people in her life . . . just the way it should be.

But then why did she feel so lonely?

Piper groaned again and stomped to her room, pulling off her sling as she went to change out of the PJ's she'd lived in for the past few days. After pulling on a pair of jeans and a comfy tunic, she ran around the house, tidying up, shutting down her large desktop computer and tucking the myriad of cords away. The house could use a thorough dusting and who knew when the bathroom had last been cleaned . . . But there wasn't time to do everything and she only had so much energy.

If only she could keep the house clean, her parents would love her . . . if only she were prettier, her parents would love her . . . if only she were popular, talked more, didn't have deadbeat parents, people would like her. . . .

If onlys were ugly things.

The ring of the doorbell called her thoughts to a halt. This was Ezra. He didn't care if she was or wasn't any of those things. He was like Paul.

Like Paul.

She sniffed and banished those thoughts as she strode across the living room to reach the entryway. Pulling the door open, she was greeted by Ezra's grin and the garlic-and-oregano scent of pizza.

Ezra hefted the pizza boxes into view and spoke. "I come bearing pizza!"

"Even if you didn't have visible proof, I could still smell them. Come on in."

He laughed and stepped past her, followed by The Incredible Hulk himself. Piper's eyes widened as she caught sight of Ezra's friend. He was even wearing a forest-green sweatshirt. Ezra spoke up from behind her. "Piper, this is my partner and buddy, Tyler Collens. Ty, Piper Redding."

Tyler Collens was a solid, six-foot-three hunk of humanity with blond hair and mischievous blue eyes, a contrast to Ezra's slimmer build and dark hair. Piper offered her hand to shake, but with a roguish grin, Tyler took it and kissed the back of it.

"Pleasure to meet you, ma'am."

She laughed. "The pleasure is mine. I think."

Tyler chuckled and Ezra shook his head. "Now you know the knucklehead. You'll probably be sorry I ever introduced you."

Piper just giggled and pushed the door closed against the softly falling snow and led them towards the kitchen. She pulled dishes from the cupboard as Ezra opened the pizza boxes and Tyler deposited himself on a dining chair as if he owned the place. As she stretched to reach an upper shelf for drinking glasses, she unconsciously used her left arm. She barely contained a groan, settling for a grimace instead, but Ezra was too perceptive. He gently nudged her out of the way and pulled the glasses out of the cabinet for her. "Where's your sling?" he asked in the scolding tone she was all-too-familiar with. Ezra had always had a tendency to play mother hen.

"Um. I took it off and forgot to put it back on."

Ezra tsked teasingly. "Now, what happens if you slip and fall and tear your stitches out? Don't expect me to be taking you to the hospital again."

Piper could feel her face turning red. "Funny you should say that . . ."

He rounded to face her. "Piper Redding, what did you do?!"

"Nothing!" she protested. "It was all the sling's fault. I took it off to rest for a bit, and it tripped me when I tried to stand up."

"It tripped you . . ."

She nodded.

Ezra laughed, as did Tyler. "I've missed the Redding family humor. Are you okay, though?" His tone turned serious.

She grinned up at him. "Peachy. And before you ask, I didn't pull out any stitches."

"Splendid. Now go put that traitorous sling back on and don't take it off again."

Piper gave a mock salute. "Bossy." Bantering with him felt so natural, as if nothing had happened in the last nine years. She'd rather missed the camaraderie of having a friend.

She walked to her room to grab the sling as Tyler piped up.

"You tell him! He's the bossiest man alive. Maybe he'll listen to you because he sure doesn't listen to me!"

"Well, he never has in the past, but maybe he'll take pity on me now that I'm injured," Piper shot over her shoulder.

Ezra shook his head in exasperation. "Not a chance. And I'm not bossy." Sending a glare to his friend, he added, "And stop talking about me like I'm not here. Or you won't get any pizza."

Tyler turned his back on Ezra and faced Piper, jerking a thumb over his shoulder. "See? What'd I tell ya?"

She giggled and shook her head as she tugged on the sling. Ezra slapped pizza onto plates and set them on the table as Tyler continued to harass him.

Maybe having friends wasn't such a bad idea. . . .

No. Piper slammed the lid on that thought before it even finished percolating. Loving someone invariably meant that they would leave someday and leave her alone . . . again. It was better to just not love, then no one could hurt you. She didn't need people and they clearly didn't need her. And that was that.

She sat down at the table and Ezra offered his hand. She stared at it, then his face for a brief few seconds before placing her hand in his. Of course he would presume to ask the blessing over their meal. He would take for granted that that was what she did. And she had. Until she'd realized the futility of praying to One who didn't listen. It was like trying to talk to her parents.

After Ezra finished the short prayer, they dug in and Tyler launched into telling funny stories about their job. Piper only half-listened, distractedly inserting forced chuckles when needed. She hadn't realized she'd zoned out completely until Ezra tapped her forehead.

"Earth to Piper—helloo, anyone home?"

"Oh, I'm—I'm sorry, what were you saying?" She looked back and forth between the two men, both of whom were looking at her with an odd look on their faces. "What?" She flushed under their scrutiny.

"Are you feeling okay?" Ezra asked.

"I'm fine, I just . . . my head hurts a little." Piper inwardly winced at the white lie. Tyler just stood up and threw away the pizza boxes, but Ezra studied her for a moment more, looking like he didn't quite believe it. He was a paramedic, after all.

She pushed to her feet. "Thank you guys for coming over and bringing pizza. I appreciated the company." Well, she did, even if she wasn't going to let it happen again.

"Our pleasure," Ezra said. "Feel free to text me if you need anything. Like another pizza fix."

She smiled. "Thanks. I will." She turned to Tyler, "It was nice to meet you, Tyler."

He gave a cheeky grin. "You too, m'lady."

She saw them out the door with a final goodbye, then closed it and sagged against it. Now she really did have a headache. Her heart and mind were waging a war, and she finally admitted a fact she'd been shoving away for so long.

She was lonely.

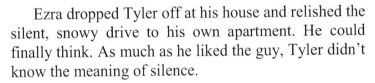

Ezra dropped Tyler off at his house and relished the silent, snowy drive to his own apartment. He could finally think. As much as he liked the guy, Tyler didn't know the meaning of silence.

He hadn't realized until today how much he missed Piper. She'd been like a little sister to him. Both being three years older, he and Paul had almost equally shared the big brother role. They were her protectors, her confidants, and her counselors. He remembered a time when her sixteen-year-old-self had come to Paul's house from school in tears because of some jerks who had teased her mercilessly.

He always did hate to see her cry.

Paul had been all for taking names and beating the bullies up—he'd been absolutely livid—but Ezra just patted her back and told her to ignore them—they didn't know what they were talking about anyway.

They were their own little family.

Between Paul and Piper's all-but-abusive parents and Ezra's terminally-ill mother, Paul's apartment became a safe haven for the three friends. There was peace and laughter . . . and Ezra didn't have to watch his mother die a little more every day.

He shook his head to clear the memories and turned his thoughts to the more recent past. Piper had all but shoved them out the door. That wasn't like her at all. She'd seemed fine at first, even ganging up on him with Tyler. But then she'd been near-silent throughout the meal and ended the impromptu lunch abruptly. She'd claimed to have a headache, but Ezra wasn't buying it. He racked his brain trying to think of something he or Ty might have said to cause the sharp change and the sudden hardness to fill her clear brown eyes.

It was almost as if she had erected a wall. As if . . . as if she were protecting herself, shutting herself in. Protecting herself from . . . him? Or from people in general?

He sighed and switched off the ignition after pulling into his designated spot under the carport at his apartment complex. He stood staring out across the field to the distant mountains behind the buildings, letting the cold wind whip snowflakes around him, cutting through his down jacket. He didn't want to be pushy, but he wanted to help Piper. It was clear her brother's death had changed her from the Piper he knew into something different. . . .

Death had a way of doing that.

But he didn't think she'd let him in. If she was set on that path, she was set to self-destruct. He would know. After his mother's death, he'd locked everyone out—his father, his friends . . . even God.

But then he'd reached rock-bottom, and it was a time he never wanted to experience again—a time of utter loneliness and despair where he'd actually considered taking his own life. Thank God for his father, who helped him get straight again.

He'd do anything to keep someone else from reaching that point, especially Piper. He couldn't let her, no matter how hard she tried to push him away. No matter how deep inside she locked herself up.

And he couldn't help but feel that it was partially his fault. . . .

Ezra whispered a prayer into the wind before turning and trudging up the steps to his apartment. It was one p.m. and he was beat. As he reached the top of the steps, he heard a strange mewling sound. He stopped, turned, and cocked his head, listening. There it was again, coming from the far corner of the dark hallway. He stepped closer, and two tiny green eyes peered out of the shadows. Pulling his cell phone out of his pocket, he flicked the flashlight app on. It illuminated a tiny, scrawny, tiger-calico cat cowering in the shadows, mewling loudly, mournfully. Who'd leave such a tiny cat all alone in a hallway? It couldn't have been more than eight weeks old. But perhaps the better questions was, what was a cat doing in a no-pets apartment building?

He sighed, realizing he didn't have a choice. This was not going to be fun, but he couldn't very well leave it there. Scooping it up, he held it in one hand, as far from his face as possible. He could already feel his eyes starting to itch—or maybe it was just his imagination.

Even though this was a no-pets building, he'd ask the neighbors if it was their kitten. After knocking on the last door and receiving the same emphatic denial of any knowledge of the cat, Ezra groaned in frustration. Now what? If he kept it—at least until he found a home for it—he would be sneezing his head off in a matter of hours—or minutes. But what other choice did he have? He blew out a breath through pursed lips and glanced at the kitten, curled up contentedly in his palm, soaking up his heat, a purr trying to rumble. "This is all your fault, you know. You're just trouble . . . in fact, that's what I'll call you—Trouble." He grunted. "Fitting." Then rolled his eyes. Twenty-nine years old, and he was talking to a cat.

He stalked to his door and fished the key out of his pocket. After letting himself in and locking the door again, he surveyed his pristine home, then looked at the cat again. He gingerly set the kitten—Trouble—right in front of the door. "Now stay. I'll be right back."

He jogged to the spare bedroom and dug through the mess therein until he found a large cardboard box. "Aha!" Grabbing it, he jogged back to the door where he'd left the kitten. The kitten that was nowhere in sight.

Letting loose an exaggerated groan, he ran a hand down his face, then stared at it as he realized what he'd done. He turned and washed his hands and face thoroughly in the kitchen sink. This afternoon was not going how he'd wanted it to. All he wanted to do was go to bed and sleep after a long workday, and instead, he was chasing a kitten—one he very much didn't want—around his apartment. He pulled an antihistamine bottle out of the cabinet and downed two tablets to stave off the allergy symptoms he knew were about two seconds from hitting en masse. He then pulled on a pair of latex gloves and dropped to his hands and knees.

"Psst, Trouble! Here, kitty! Where did you GO?" He managed to keep the first part of his sentence coaxing, but it had become angry by the last words. If anyone heard him yelling at a cat . . . he'd be doubly in trouble. Both with his landlord and his neighbors, who would undoubtedly think him crazy. He blew out a breath and continued his search.

"Ah! There you are, you little . . . thing." He plucked the kitten up off the couch pillow it had decided to curl up on and carried it over to the box he had found.

"There. Now you're not going anywhere." He sneezed and the kitten looked up at him and mewed pitifully. "Don't you dare look at me like that!" He was too much of a softie for his own good. Ezra scrounged up an old sheet and put it on the box, then poured some milk in a dish and some canned chicken in another and put those in the box as well.

"There. Now stop complaining." The little kitten dug into the food as if it hadn't seen any in days—which it probably hadn't. He watched it for a moment, then grunted. "A thank you would be nice."

Now he was going to bed.

He sneezed, then blinked as his eyes watered.

After tossing and turning—and sneezing—all afternoon, Ezra finally strode into work, bleary-eyed and with a pack of tissues in his pocket. He caught Tyler's eye and the man did a double take before walking over to him.

"Whoa, dude, you look like something the cat dragged in. What happened?"

"A cat drug me in. Dragged me in? Whatever." Ezra chuckled. Tyler sent him a concerned look and he sighed. "I found a kitten outside my apartment when I got home, and of course, I couldn't just leave it there."

"Of course," was all Tyler said, but Ezra had a feeling he was barely restraining a hearty laugh at his expense.

"I need to find a home for it, as this—" he waved a hand in the general direction of his own face— "is not going to work."

Tyler, again restraining a chuckle, nodded and looked thoughtful.

Ezra continued. "I was thinking maybe one of the families at church would want a kitten."

Tyler's eyes lit up. "Hey! What about asking Piper What's-her-name if she wants to take it? She seems like the type of gal who would love a kitten in the house."

Ezra smacked his forehead. "Of course! Why didn't I think of it?" Tyler's conjecture wasn't actually that far off. She would always be bringing wounded and neglected animals off the streets of the Chicago suburbs home with her. Until her parents put a stop to it. Then she started bringing them to Paul. "I'll take it to her first thing tomorrow."

"Great. Now go take an allergy tablet or something. You look like a freak."

Ezra sent his friend a glare, but its effects were probably minimized by his red, swollen eyes. "Wow. Thanks a lot, friend."

Tyler slapped him on the back before turning to finish his coffee. "No problemo, man."

Piper groggily pushed herself out of bed. Sleep was overrated. Who needed sleep? Not if it was riddled with nightmares. These ones were different though. Instead of being about her brother, Ezra was in them, too. He and Paul—and Tyler was there somewhere too; she heard his laugh—were walking away from her, laughing, paying no attention to her as she screamed at them to come back. She wanted to chase after them, but something pinned her arms, held her in place.

She shook her head. Sleep was definitely overrated. Pulling her bathrobe on, she plodded to the kitchen, wishing she drank coffee. The caffeine would be appreciated right now. Instead, she made herself a mug of hot cocoa, the need for comfort stronger than the need for energy.

Mug in hand, she curled up on the couch with one of her favorite historical novels. Peace settled her mind and heart at the familiarity of routine and the homelike comfort of her favorite drink and story combined. The Christmas lights she kept up year round twinkled at her cheerily, brightening her mood. Maybe today wouldn't be such a wretched day after all. If she ignored the grogginess from the sleepless night and the slight throbbing in her shoulder, she could pretend that everything was normal.

That she wasn't shot a week ago.

That her brother's best friend hadn't shown up, bringing with him a passel of memories and guilt that she thought she'd buried years ago.

That she wasn't lonely—that she was happy being alone. . . .

That there wasn't a black hole in her heart that used to be filled by love, light, laughter and peace—all things that had abandoned her on the twenty-second of January, six years ago.

Pretending was easier than facing reality.

So Piper finished her drink and book, took a shower, got dressed and sat down at her computer to work, although it was difficult to do so with her dominant hand still in a sling. She was just about finished putting the final touches on a new corporate client's website. Which meant a large check with her name on it would be arriving soon, and the first thing she planned to do was go to the Barnes and Noble in town and splurge on at least three new books she'd been looking forward to reading—maybe a few more. Thankfully she'd be able to drive by then.

She buckled down to finish the task and was nearly finished when a knock interrupted her concentration. She pushed herself upright from her hunched position squinting at the monitor. Who would be knocking at this hour? She checked her watch. 9:30.

Taking the few steps from her corner desk to the door, she pulled it open and her eyes widened. "Ezra? What are you doing here? Are you okay?" He stood with his hands behind his back, his face red and eyes puffy and bloodshot.

He grimaced. "I'm fine. Or I will be. But I need your help."

"My help?" Confusion was undoubtedly written all over her face.

"Yes, but may I come in?"

"Oh!" Piper pulled the door open wider and stepped aside, shivering in the cool wind that blew in along with Ezra. He sneezed into his shoulder, then held out the item he'd been holding behind his back—a small box—to her. She sent him another confused look as she took it, but he just grinned, offering no explanation.

She opened the box. And blinked. "Oh, Ezra . . . ," she breathed. Scooping up the tiny kitten, she cradled it against her chest and dropped the box. Gray, white, and tan mixed in splashes across the scrawny kitten's back, and it mewed softly, then purred, a barely audible sputtering that sounded like a reluctant motor starting up. Piper looked up at Ezra. "Where did you get her?"

He had his hands stuffed in his pockets, a shy grin on his face. "My apartment building hallway, believe it or not. I couldn't just leave it there with how cold it's been."

"Aw! You're such a softie." The kitten nosed around in her hands and Piper let it climb up onto her shoulder where it sat, surveying her new surroundings.

Ezra laughed. "I think that title belongs to you."

She sent him a bittersweet smile, remembering all the times Paul had lovingly accused her of being too soft-hearted. "Yeah, I guess."

"Anyway, I couldn't keep it because my apartment has a no pets rule, not to mention, I'm allergic to cats." He grimaced again and rubbed his eyes. He didn't look like he got much sleep last night either.

"So Ty suggested I give it to you."

"Her," she corrected.

He blinked. "How do you know it's a her?"

Piper rolled her eyes. "It's obvious. She's a calico, and all calicos are female."

"Oh." There was silence for a few moments as they both watched the kitten clamber over Piper. Ezra cleared his throat. "I thought maybe I could take you to the store to get whatever you need for it—her?"

Piper's eyes widened at his suggestion. "Oh!" Wait. No. Well . . . Piper's desire to get out of the house after being cooped up for days won out over her reluctance to spending time with Ezra. Simply knowing she couldn't drive made her all the more restless. "Actually, that'd be great. Thanks. I do need some groceries too, if you don't mind."

"Not at all." He smiled, his green eyes crinkling at the corners in a way that was so familiar.

She glanced down at her casual tunic and leggings. "I'll be right back. You can hold—never mind." She started to give the kitten over to Ezra before stopping and putting the kitten back in the box she'd come in and setting it by the couch. "Help yourself to a drink or something. I'll only be a minute," she called over her shoulder as she headed to her room.

Closing the door behind her, she quickly threw on a pair of jeans and a nicer tunic, pulled her medium-length red-brown hair into a low side pony, and grabbed her purse, tossing a few items in it. She glanced in the mirror and grimaced at the dark circles under her eyes. She looked like a racoon. But nothing to be done for it. She left her room and Ezra turned from perusing the floor-to-ceiling bookshelves that lined a portion of the living room wall.

"You look nice."

She laughed. "Ha! But that's sweet of you to say."

"No, I'm serious!" he insisted, face earnest. She just rolled her eyes and quickly swallowed two of the pain pills. But a tiny spot in her heart thawed a little. Nobody—except maybe Paul—ever complimented her and actually seemed genuine.

"Ready?"

"Mmhm." Piper pulled her coat on, leaving her left arm still in a sling inside of the coat. Giving the now-sleeping kitten a parting pat on the head, she pulled the door open and let Ezra pass before locking it and closing it behind her. Carefully maneuvering her way across the icy driveway, she looked up to see Ezra holding the passenger's side door of his car open for her.

"Thanks," she mumbled as she slid in. He just smiled and shut the door behind her, then climbed in on his own side and pulled out of the drive.

After a few minutes of silence, he asked, "How's your shoulder doing?"

She shrugged and sat her purse on the floor at her feet. "Pretty good, I guess. Mostly just throbs a lot. I can't wait till I can drive again. I feel so cooped up knowing I can't." Why was she rambling? *Stop rambling.*

Ezra tsked sympathetically. "Just give it another week or so. Your muscles got torn up pretty badly."

She nodded and watched the tall, snow-covered pines pass in a whir as they left the outskirts of town behind. "So what should I name the kitten?"

He slanted her a glance. "Well, I named it Trouble . . ."

Piper choked on her laughter and a grin slid across Ezra's face. "What kind of name is that?!"

"A fitting one, after all the trouble she gave me."

Piper shook her head. "You can't name a sweet little thing like her that!"

"Fine then, name her something cute like Fluffles," Ezra shot back.

"I don't do cutesy." She rolled her eyes.

Ezra chuckled and shook his head. "Of course not."

Piper just made a face at him and turned back to the window. It struck her again how familiar their banter felt. It felt like old times—better times. Happy times. A sigh escaped her.

"What?"

She started. "Oh, um . . . nothing really. How about Finley?"

He tilted his head side to side as if weighing it in his mind. "Sure, I like it. It's sophisticated, old fashioned. Like you. It fits."

"Hey! Watch what you're saying, Ezra Bryant," she scolded with a light slap on his arm. His laugh echoed and she found herself grinning.

For the moment, at least, she felt happy. It was a freeing feeling.

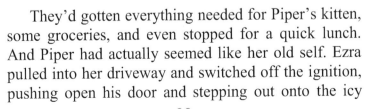

They'd gotten everything needed for Piper's kitten, some groceries, and even stopped for a quick lunch. And Piper had actually seemed like her old self. Ezra pulled into her driveway and switched off the ignition, pushing open his door and stepping out onto the icy pavement. He heard a light squeal and jerked back around to find Piper gone. Rushing around the front of the car, he found her sitting on the slick concrete, a pained expression on her face.

"Whoa, you okay?" He squatted next to her.

She winced and nodded. "I think so . . . I can't seem to stay on my feet lately. Ice is slippery, by the way."

He chuckled and pushed to his feet. "At least you still have your sense of humor." Grasping her good arm and placing his other hand on her waist, he smoothly pulled her to her feet, noting how small she was. "You're sure you're okay?" he asked again, still keeping a grip on her arm. She sent him a look that bespoke sass and extricated her arm from his.

"I hurt my pride, not my legs, Ezra."

He laughed. "If you say so. You go see to Finley. I'll get the stuff out of the back."

Piper cautiously turned towards the house, and he pulled the grocery sacks full of items out of the trunk and brought them in. Setting them on her dining room table, he turned and found her standing behind him, Finley purring contentedly in her arms.

"Thank you so much for today, Ezra. It was nice to get out of the house for a bit." Her smile was sincere and gratitude softened the stressed lines of her face.

He shrugged self-consciously. "Anytime. I didn't have anything better to do with my morning anyway."

Piper nodded, then studied him thoughtfully, hand still methodically stroking Finley. "I never asked. How is your dad?"

"Oh, he's good. He's got a great job, and loves it, so, yeah. He's doing good."

She nodded again, then looked down before meeting his eyes, her own now shaded. "You both left so suddenly after . . . well, you know." She looked down at the kitten again, avoiding his eyes. His heart clenched at the memory of what she was alluding to, and he shifted uncomfortably, his eyes wandering around the room. He looked back at her and found her shimmering brown eyes drilling into him with an intensity he hadn't seen before.

"Why?" she murmured. "Why didn't you say goodbye?"

Ezra's gut twisted. Because he'd been drunk on pain, on anger. And other substances. But he couldn't tell her that. Any of it. He reached out and rested his hand on her arm. "I'm so sorry, Piper." His voice cracked on her name, and the disappointment clouding her eyes felt like a literal blow to his diaphragm.

He couldn't. Not now.

He stepped around her and let himself out, jogging down the driveaway. Getting in his car, he turned onto the street as his heart beat to the tune of *failure, failure, failure.*

His father's voice filtered above the noise of his heart in clear relief.

"You gotta stop running from the pain, Ezra. You have to face it like a man and only then will it go away."

But he couldn't face it. Couldn't face her. Not about this. The pain and disgust that would fill her eyes if he told her would be far worse than the disappointment that filled them today.

Stop running, Ez . . . stop running.

He knew God had forgiven him of his past and didn't hold it against him.

But that didn't mean Piper would do the same.

7

iper stood unmoving as the door softly clicked shut behind Ezra and his footsteps sounded down the driveway.

Alone. Again.

The kitten in her arms meowed, and Piper realized she'd been unconsciously squeezing her. "Sorry, Finley. I shouldn't take it out on you. You weren't the one who left." Finley just licked Piper's fingers in reconciliation, and she giggled. "Guess you're hungry."

She poured some of the food they'd bought into a small dish and set it on the floor next to the kitten. Finley eagerly dug in and Piper put away the groceries, settled the kitten bed in her room, and tucked the cat food on a shelf in the garage.

Piper stood with her hand on her hip and blew out a breath. Now what? She'd really enjoyed the time with Ezra . . . until his strange reaction to her simple question.

She had a right to know why he left so suddenly all those years ago. Paul wouldn't tell her, just saying that Ezra and his dad had needed some space after Ezra's mom had died. It still didn't give a person a reason to leave and not say goodbye to friends. Paul had admitted that Ezra hadn't said goodbye to him either. He hadn't even told him where he was going.

He had just abandoned them like everyone else had done in her life . . . She heaved a sigh. Was there anyone she could trust? Maybe it was her fault every person in her life walked out.

All your fault . . . the mocking voice had taken up residence in her mind again. Tears burned behind her eyes as the three words echoed tauntingly through the corridors of her mind. She clenched her teeth and fists against them.

"It's not my fault!" Her yell sent Finley scrambling for safety and the tears flowing in earnest. She sank onto the sofa and pulled her knees up against her chest, burrowing her face in them. The tears soaked the knees of her jeans. How long? How long would the voices in her head taunt her? How long would the pain and guilt settle like a rock on her chest, making it so hard to breathe?

"I just want peace, God. Peace," she muttered into her knees. She sat there, shaking as the sobs wracked her body, letting her mind and heart slowly grow numb. It was easier to ignore the elephant sitting on her chest than address it.

So that's what she'd do.

Flopping sideways on the couch, she pulled the fuzzy throw blanket over her body. Finley came out of hiding and cuddled up against her as she closed her eyes. Soon her breathing grew regular as a restless sleep of exhaustion overtook her body.

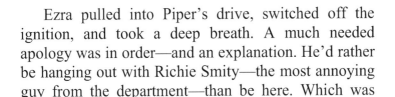

Ezra pulled into Piper's drive, switched off the ignition, and took a deep breath. A much needed apology was in order—and an explanation. He'd rather be hanging out with Richie Smity—the most annoying guy from the department—than be here. Which was saying a lot.

He'd put it off for two days already. Sucking in another deep breath, he started up the walk to her front door. He raised a hand to knock, but paused when the muted sounds of mumbling came through the door. The TV perhaps? Although it didn't sound like it. Frowning, he knocked and when there was no answer, knocked again. He turned the knob and found it was unlocked. Pushing the door open, he prayed he wasn't making a mistake. But he knew there was a reason he was here.

He peered around the corner of the entryway into the main area. The house was silent except for thrashing and muted mumblings coming from the couch.

"Piper?" he called softly. No answer. He gulped and glanced behind him. Well, he couldn't really leave now. He stepped into the room and dropped to a knee by the couch. Her mumblings morphed into actual words.

"Please don't leave me! You can't leave! Somebody help him!"

Ezra swallowed down the emotion her pitiful tone raised. She was having a nightmare. Gripping her good arm, he gently shook her. "Piper? Piper, it's just a dream; wake up."

Her eyes shot open and she blinked into his face once before launching herself into an upright position, the sudden movement startling him and causing him to backpedal two steps. She fixed him with a wide-eyed stare, her eyes still glossy and unfocused. "Paul?" she croaked.

A tiny crack appeared in his heart. He shook his head and spoke softly, soothingly, placing the back of his hand against her forehead. "No, it's me, Ezra." No fever.

Recognition dawned in her now-clear eyes before she closed them and leaned her head back against the couch with a groan. Silence stretched between them only broken by Piper's ragged breathing.

This was a bad idea.

Finally Ezra cleared his throat and spoke. "I'm sorry, I knocked but you didn't answer and I heard . . . and the door was unlocked, so . . ." he finished lamely and shrugged.

She lifted her head up and shook it. "It's all right. Thanks . . . thanks for waking me up." She shook her head again as if to clear it of the dream. Then cleared her throat. "Why'd you come over?"

"I . . ." Well, he couldn't very well bring up the topic he had planned on now. "I just thought you might like some company and I wasn't working today, and I know you don't know anyone else around Arlington."

A smile quirked up her lips and the room seemed to lighten. "Except Cecile. She was a sweetheart. Gave me her phone number and told me to call if I ever needed anything. She's the only person I know here." Her words were spoken in a wistful tone.

"Well, you know me. We go way back." Ezra grinned.

She gave a slight chuckle and the way she looked at him made him wonder if she wished she didn't know him. Or something. He was never good at interpreting women's facial expressions with any accuracy. They were never what they seemed, he'd learned. You'd think crying meant sad, and smiling meant happy, but somehow crying could mean happy too . . . so maybe it was just better not to assume. "Piper, if you'd rather I didn't come over, then that's fine. I understand."

She abruptly looked up from her lap and met his eyes, startled. "No! I mean, no, it's fine. It was very thoughtful of you to come over and I . . . I like the company. It's just . . ." Her face scrunched up as she searched for words. Standing, she maneuvered through the mess of computer cords and cables and stray pillows scattered across the floor to stand at the window. It looked like an electrician—or maybe just a tech geek—had had a heyday in her living room.

Ezra stood and shoved his hands in his pockets and waited for her to finish her sentence. "It's just . . . ?" he prompted.

"It's just you . . . he . . ." she sighed. "You remind me of Paul," she whispered. "I've done such a good job of burying the memories away in the furthest corners of my mind. It's how I cope. But with this—" she gestured to her shoulder "—and you, everything's unraveling and it just hurts, Ezra. It hurts." Her voice broke on the last words.

The silence was unbroken after Piper's rambling confession. He didn't know what to say. "I'm sorry, Piper," he whispered.

At Ezra's softly spoken words, something cracked and the dam she'd tried so hard to shore up broke loose.

Silently, sobs shook her body and all the grief, pain, and guilt she'd tried so hard to bury welled up and overwhelmed her. What was wrong with her? Spilling her guts to a practical stranger—regardless of whether said stranger had been basically a brother at one point in her life. And now crying? Piper tried vainly to stop the emotion and lock it back up tight, but as water rushing from opened floodgates can't be stopped, neither would the tears.

The next thing she knew she was enveloped in a giant, but soft, bear hug. The kindness behind the gesture only made the tears flow faster.

Finally, the well ran dry. Piper felt so empty. But maybe that was better than the lead that had weighed her down before. Ezra took a step back out of the hug and after a glance at her face, grabbed an entire box of tissues off the nearby end table and handed it to her. She gave a broken chuckle and sniffed. "That bad, huh?"

He just grinned and gently pushed her to sit on the couch. Then, grabbing up the sling she'd taken off and deposited on the floor, he guided her arm into it with practiced care. "Leave that on," he instructed with a stern look.

She swallowed and mopped her face with her other hand. "Yes, doctor."

He patted the top of her head condescendingly and strolled off towards the kitchen. She heard the sounds of the water kettle boiling and the thump of mugs hitting the counter. She sniffled against the tears that wanted to erupt again and leaned her head against the back of the couch. Why was he being so nice?

She closed her eyes and took a deep breath. Flashbacks of the nightmare floated through her mind with startling clarity. She tried to shut them out, but couldn't. The red was seeping everywhere. . . .

Heart beating wildly, Piper opened her eyes and started counting the blue books on the shelf on the opposite wall. Anything but the red ones. . . .

Ezra poked his head out of the kitchen and asked, "No coffee?"

She shook her head.

He popped back into the kitchen muttering something about coffee in an incredulous tone. Two minutes later he showed up with two mugs of tea and handed her one. Peppermint. She grimaced slightly and held it in her lap. A tin of it was in the box of food Ezra had brought. She thought she'd thrown it away.

Ezra took a seat across from her with his own mug and took a sip, doing a double take into the mug with a wrinkle in his brow. Apparently peppermint tea wasn't his thing either. But it was the thought that counted. He looked up at her. "Want to talk about it?"

"About what?"

He raised an eyebrow at her facetious response and answered in kind. "It."

She set aside her mug. "How about we talk about why you left." Wait, did she really want to talk about that right now? Yes. She wanted answers. She kept her head down but peeked up at his face and saw his eyes darken and his jaw tighten. A muscle in his cheek throbbed with the tension and he stared at his mug of tea as if it contained answers within.

Clearing his throat, he finally spoke. "That's actually why I came . . . I wanted to apologize for leaving so abruptly earlier . . . well, the other day. I'm sorry, that was rude. I . . . I—" he sighed. "I'm sorry, Piper."

She leaned forward, clenching her hands together. "But what about nine years ago?"

Ezra set his mug on the end table and pushed to his feet, paced to the window and stared out at the frozen landscape, his back to her. His shoulders were rigid and his arms folded across his chest. Then he turned and faced her, meeting her eyes. "Because I was stupid." Shame flushed his squared jaw and he walked back to sit next to her. "After my mom died, I . . . lost it. I was mad at myself, God, my mom, my dad." He snorted. "Pretty much everyone who was anyone. My grades started tanking and my instructors threatened to expel me. And . . ." he swallowed hard and looked down. "I started drinking. Man, was I messed up. Dad and Paul tried to help, but I just ignored them. One night, I came home, stoned." Piper stiffened and he grabbed her hand, clutching it tightly, his eyes begging her to understand. He shook his head. "Paul didn't want you to know . . .

And he told me to get it together or leave. He said he'd help me, but that I had to want it. I didn't want it, then . . . I just wanted to numb the pain. I was barely existing, let alone living. So my dad and I packed up and moved here. He thought the fresh start would be good for both of us." He paused and drew in a deep breath.

"Was it?" Piper asked softly.

"No. Yes. It made me realize what I'd lost. What I'd wasted. I felt like I blew it. I didn't think there was anything worth living for . . ." His voice cracked and the full import of his words sunk in. "I almost killed myself," he whispered, agony in his eyes.

"Oh, Ezra . . . ," she breathed, tears slowly trickling down her face.

"My dad . . ." He cleared his throat and started again. "My dad saved my life. And he helped me turn it back around. He loved me through the worst time of my life, and that's when I knew it was going to be okay." Tears now tracked down his cheeks as well. "Eventually I finished school, got a job. Got right with God . . . I never want to go back to that place again," he choked out.

Piper's heart cracked at the depth of pain he'd gone through. And she'd never known. She scooted closer and wrapped her arms around his waist. He hesitated before folding his arms around her, burying his face on her shoulder. She felt shudders wrack his body and tightened her grip.

She didn't know how long they sat there like that before Ezra finally drew back. He ran a hand over his face and seemed to wipe away the memories. He went back to his chair across from her and picked up his mug of now-cold tea, staring silently into it. Piper just waited, sensing there was more he wanted to say. Finally, he set the mug on the end table and met her eyes again.

"I'm sorry for leaving, Piper. I'm sorry for not saying goodbye. I'm sorry for not being there when . . . when Paul died." His voice cracked again and Piper closed her eyes against the threatening of tears again.

The pain was almost tangible, and Piper's heart throbbed dully at the reminder of Paul.

"Why?" she forced out. "If God is so good, then why is there so much pain, so much death in this world?"

Ezra knelt in front of her and gripped her hands tightly, compelling her to look at him. She did and the raw earnestness in them surprised her. "Piper, He is good. He's sovereign, but there are natural consequences to our sin. But that doesn't mean He's not good. He is, Piper. I've seen it. I've seen it and felt it in the depths of my soul, that He is good. He saved my life. He redeemed me, even after I'd messed things up so badly. He loves us, Piper. And He's good. I know it's hard to believe that, 'cause I've been there too, but He is." Moisture sparkled in his clear green eyes that begged her to believe him. To believe. And she wanted to—she wanted to so badly—but she wasn't sure her heart could handle any more disappointments if Ezra was wrong. . . .

Ezra peered into Piper's eyes, and felt that he could see the very depths of her heart . . . she was terrified. Terrified to be hurt again. He could see the fear, the guilt, the pain. And his heart clenched, wishing he could take it all away. Wishing he could fix it, make it all better. Help her somehow. But he knew there was nothing more he could do right now. And that hurt.

Except pray. *Father, heal her hurt. Heal her heart.*

He stood and gently tugged her to her feet, wrapping his arms around her again. She felt small, fragile, able to break at the slightest impact. And he knew she was. "It's okay, Piper. It's okay," he murmured, softly rubbing her back and feeling the tension slip away. He eased back to look at her and was worried by the hollow look in her eyes. "Hey. Are you okay?" he asked softly.

She nodded and took a deep breath. "I'm fine."

He was doubtful, but nodded back anyway, and squeezed her shoulder. "I should get going." He took their mugs to the sink and rinsed them before pulling on his jacket. He looked at her once more before turning toward the door. Her softly spoken words had him pausing, hand on the doorknob.

"Thank you, Ez."

He turned and gave her a smile, inwardly grinning at her use of his nickname. "Bye, Piper."

His heart was heavy as he drove home. The protector in him wanted to take away all that had hurt Piper, erase it from her memory. All the pain she'd been through had made her close off her heart, keeping her from loving or trusting anyone. Not even God. Perhaps Him most of all.

He just felt so helpless . . . He wanted to pound a wall.

Failure. Again.

He parked his car in the apartment lot and pulled the key out, then tugged his phone out of his pocket. Pulling up the correct message thread, he sent off a text asking if he could drop by after his dad got out of the office. Tucking his phone into his back pocket, he scrubbed a hand across his face and blew out a breath. Grabbing his duffel, he headed up the steps to his apartment.

He needed sleep, first and foremost.

Live Without You

Pain settled deep in Piper's heart, but it was a different kind of pain, a dull, aching, throbbing pain. A longing for something she didn't have. Couldn't have.

She wished Ezra had stayed, yet she knew she wouldn't have let him. His mere presence was slowly breaking down her bleak concrete walls . . . and it terrified her. She'd told him so much today. More than she meant to. She wasn't sure yet if she regretted it. In a way, it felt freeing to share the burden with someone else, but he didn't even know the half of it. . . .

Would it be so terrible to let him break down those walls? Her head said it would, but her heart suggested that maybe it was worth the risk.

◆

Ezra gratefully accepted the cup of liquid caffeine from his dad. It would certainly come in handy later as the last hours of his shift stretched long. And no one made coffee like his dad. He inhaled deeply of the fresh, earthy scent and felt instantly calmer. His dad settled himself with his own mug across from Ezra and propped an ankle on his knee. He had shed the suit jacket and cufflinks and loosened his tie, but otherwise was still in his office attire.

Tom Bryant cut an imposing figure at just around six feet tall with black hair turning salt-and-pepper, and the square face and green eyes he shared with Ezra. As a civil litigation attorney, he could be quite intimidating, but Ezra knew there was a soft heart of gold underneath, and he was every inch a gentleman.

After a few minutes of comfortable silence, Ezra looked up and found his dad studying him with a contemplative look in his gentle eyes.

"What?" he asked, slightly defensive.

His dad chuckled, clearly bemused. "You tell me, Ezra. You didn't just show up here without a reason."

Ezra laughed ruefully. "I see why you're so good at your job."

"Nope, I just know my son well."

Ezra smiled softly and nodded, staring into his already nearly empty mug. "So . . . I came across Piper Redding the other day . . ."

"Paul Redding's sister? Why did I have a feeling this was going to be about a girl?"

"Da-ad!" Now his father was jumping on that bandwagon too? His dad was biting the inside of his cheek, clearly trying to restrain himself from a laugh at his son's expense.

"Sorry, you know I was teasing." Dad coughed, still covering up a chuckle.

"You and everyone else," Ezra said, shaking his head with exasperation.

"How is Piper?" Dad asked, a more serious note in his voice.

Ezra blew out a breath. "Not good, Dad."

Alarm skittered across his father's usually impassive face at Ezra's heavy tone. "What's wrong?"

"Paul died. Years ago."

"He what—?" His dad's voice cracked and he cleared his throat. "I'm so sorry, son." He placed a hand on Ezra's shoulder and squeezed.

Ezra nodded and swallowed. Twice. His dad knew. He understood.

Ezra had never had the opportunity to apologize to Paul. And now he never would. He'd spent enough time beating himself up over past stupid decisions and missed opportunities. He wouldn't over this one. But the guilt still stung—like fire.

"He was shot in a gang fight six years ago. Died instantly." He chuckled humorlessly. "Want to know the ironic thing? Piper was shot too—last week in the shooting at the rink."

Shock splashed across his father's features. "Oh my goodness. That's terrible. She's all right though?"

Ezra nodded and explained her injury. It wasn't breaking patient confidentiality if said patient was an old friend, right? "She's really struggling, Dad. I don't know what to do, and it's killing me. I know she blames herself about Paul—she hasn't said so, but she doesn't need to. I think her getting injured brought everything to the surface. She feels like God abandoned her. I just . . . I just want to fix it!" He exhaled in frustration and dropped his head, rubbing his face with his hands.

His father was silent for a few minutes before he spoke softly. "You can't, Ez. You can't. The only thing you can do is pray for her and love her through it."

Ezra's head snapped up and he stared at his father. "Dad!" he said, aghast. Did he just say what Ezra thought he'd said?

His dad looked confused for a moment before a grin broke out and he chuckled, a rich sound. "Ezra Christopher Bryant, you know I didn't mean it that way. I meant a brotherly love. Just be there for her, but also give her some space."

Ezra exhaled loudly and Dad chuckled again. "You know, you're unusually worked up about that specific subject . . . which I have a feeling is telling."

Ezra grimaced. "You would be too, if people were constantly bringing it up. Tyler hasn't let me hear the end of it, and I'm not sure I ever will."

"It'll blow over." Dad's words were encouraging, but the not-very-hidden smirk on his face wasn't. It was rather alarming, actually. Ezra decided now would be an ideal time to change the subject. He asked his father about the case he was working on, and they continued to talk for another half hour before Ezra had to leave for work.

As Ezra made the silent drive to work, his dad's words replayed in his mind. "Just love her . . ." Maybe there was more to that than what he had meant. But not yet. Piper didn't need that.

Lord, I don't even know what to pray anymore . . . Show me how to help her. Use me.

Live Without You

When Piper awoke from a nightmare at 3:30 a.m. on January twenty-second, she knew it was going to be a horrible day.

That much she could have guessed without the waking up early part. The nightmare was a kick-you-while-you're-down kind of addition. She sighed and turned on her side, scrunching the pillow up beneath her head more comfortably.

Then it hit her. Today marked two weeks since the shooting at the rink. And six years since Paul had died . . . Oh, the irony.

She closed her eyes and tried to get back to sleep, but her mind was too awake. She rolled over to turn on the lamp and let out a squeal when Finley yowled and jumped off the bed. She must have been sleeping at Piper's back, and Piper had almost rolled over on her.

She cringed at the mental image of squashed-flat cat and stage-whispered to Finley. "Sorry, kitty! C'mere." She snapped her fingers softly, but Finley disdainfully put her nose in the air and began to clean a paw. Stubborn cat.

Piper flipped on the lamp and grabbed the book she was currently reading off the nightstand. When Crickets Cry, one of her favorites, and one she'd read many times. She read until her eyelids grew heavy. She shut them for a moment, only to open them again three hours later with a furball sitting on her neck, tail tickling her nose. Piper groaned. Did this cat have no social skills?

Grumbling, she displaced Finley and lethargically climbed out from the teal bed sheets to ready herself for the day. She was staring absentmindedly into her closet trying to decide what to wear when the shrill ringing of her phone from the bedside table startled her and sent Finley yowling and running from the room. Strangely, the sound of the phone ringing always sent the kitten for cover.

Piper grabbed the phone and frowned at the unfamiliar number. Who would be calling this early in the morning? Although it was 8:30. She cleared her throat and hoped her morning voice didn't sound too terrible as she swiped the screen to answer the call. "Hello?"

"Piper! Honey, that you?" The mellow accented voice sounded familiar.

"Um, yes, this is Piper. May I ask who's calling?"

A rich chuckle met her question. "Shoo, girl, this is Cecile."

The nurse. Duh. "Miss Cecile! How are you?"

Another chuckle. "I'm just fine, honeygirl. Listen, I thought today we could go do some shoppin', lunch, ya know, what girls do. I know you must be bored out of your *mind* all alone in that house. What d'ya say?"

"Oh, um . . . well . . ." She cleared her throat. "That would be nice. Thank you very much."

"Alrighty! Whoo! It's a date. I'll pick you up about 9:30? That sound good?"

"Lovely!" And it actually did.

"Alrighty, honeygirl. See ya then." The line clicked.

Surprisingly, Piper wasn't freaked out about a near-stranger calling and taking her shopping. It was the way Cecile talked—as if she had known you all your life and was your best friend. The small amount of time Piper had spent in it, she'd enjoyed the outgoing woman's company. And she was looking forward to getting out of the house for a bit.

She snagged a peacock-blue sweater and a pair of soft-gray jeans from the closet and pulled them on. Finger-combing her wavy bed head, she brought some semblance of order to it and pinned back the front pieces.

Makeup or no? Well, it was a girls' day after all. She applied a light layer of mascara and a coat of peachy lip gloss. Frowning at her pale cheeks, she pinched them gently. She was still so pale. The doctor had said it would take awhile for her body to replenish the blood she'd lost. It'd been two weeks, and she still looked like Frankenstein's Monster.

Piper finished getting ready and ran around the house, trying to tidy up the monstrosity it was before gulping down a muffin and a hard-boiled egg as breakfast. Finished with that, she scrolled through notifications on her phone while waiting for 9:30 and Miss Cecile to arrive.

After stopping at two stores, Piper settled herself in Miss Cecile's passenger seat again as the woman pulled out onto the main road. The pleasantries long since already gone through, there was silence except for the sound of the wheels on the wet asphalt. It was just starting to get awkward when Miss Cecile spoke.

"How are you really doin', hon?"

Piper was touched at the concern evident in Miss Cecile's voice. No one had ever asked her that question with such care, such . . . love, behind it. She sniffed against the sudden moisture in her eyes. "I'm . . . I'm doing okay, thanks."

Cecile shifted her grip on the wheel and sent a raised-eyebrows glance in Piper's direction. "Girl, you're obviously not okay, and I ain't above dragging it out of you, so you'd better start talking." Cecile's tone left no room for argument.

Piper chuckled and squirmed a bit, but surprisingly wasn't bothered by her companion's pushiness. Instead of elaborating, she decided to ask the question that had been bothering her for some time. "Why do you care?" It was softly spoken with no attitude behind it, just pained curiosity.

Cecile answered with little hesitation, clicking on her turn signal to pull into a Starbucks as she did so. "Because the One tells me to care, hon." She flicked a finger upward. "So I do. I been praying for you night and day since you showed up in my rotation. Well, if I'm being honest, I asked to have you put on my rotation. Not every day we get gunshot victims here." She winked and pulled up to the drive-thru window. "Like coffee?"

Piper blinked at the abrupt change in subject. "Um, no, I don't care for it."

Cecile feigned horror. "Not like coffee? Well, I declare. What do you like?"

"I like hot cocoa . . ." Before she finished her sentence, Cecile had turned towards the window and ordered a hot cocoa with extra whipped cream and chocolate syrup, and a "venti half-decaf half-blonde roast with room for hot water" . . . whatever that was.

Drinks in hand, Miss Cecile pulled into an empty parking space and took a sip of her strange-sounding coffee. "My momma said there ain't nothin' coffee and a lil' bit o' Jesus can't fix."

Piper sipped her drink and stared out the windshield as snowflakes slowly accumulated on it and twinkled around the buildings in the distance. "I haven't found either very effective in my personal experience," she said lightly.

"Oh? That so?" Miss Cecile took another sip of her drink, letting the words drift in the quietness.

"Yes, that's so . . . So why pray at all if God just ignores you?"

"God never ignores, honey, He just maybe doesn't answer the way we want or when we want. But He knows best, and always answers in the way that's best for us."

"Then you're saying it was God's plan that my brother bleed out in a dark, abandoned Chicago alley before medical help could reach him? How is that 'best'?" Piper couldn't help the bitterness that had crept into her tone and she hurriedly took a sip to cover the crack in her voice.

Miss Cecile made a sympathetic noise and reached out a hand and placed it over Piper's, surprising her with her acceptance after that little speech. "I didn't say it had to make sense to us. You may never know why your brother died. Things happen. But God can turn it around and use it for good if you'll let Him. Let me ask this: was your brother a Christian?"

"Yes. Very much so. He was always talking about God, and praying, and . . . he said he was praying that I would know God, too . . . but then he died. So what good did his prayers do?"

"Maybe the good God wants to bring out of his death is that you come to know God in a bigger way."

Piper was silent as she processed Miss Cecile's words.

"Somehow, I don't think that's truly what's holding you back, Piper." Miss Cecile's words startled her. How could she know? "What is it?" Cecile tapped a finger to Piper's chest. "In your heart of hearts, what's stopping you from accepting His love?"

Piper looked down at her lap where Cecile's dark, strong hand still clasped her own small one. A tear slipped down her cheek as she spoke the words that had haunted her all her life. "I'm scared, Miss Cecile. I'm scared that I've done too much for Him to love me. I'm not good enough. I'm scared that He'll leave me like everyone else. It just hurts too much." More tears followed the first one.

"I am convinced that neither death, nor life, nor angels, nor principalities, nor things present nor things to come, nor powers, nor height, nor depth, nor any other created thing, will be able to separate us from the unlimited love of God. 'For the mountains may be removed and the hills may shake, but My love will not be removed from you, nor will My covenant of peace be shaken,' says the Lord." Cecile's words had started quietly and slowly grown with strength and conviction until her voice filled the car. Faster and faster slipped the tears down Piper's face and she saw Cecile wiping away tears of her own. She gripped Piper's hand tighter. "He loves you, Piper Redding. Goodness, He's crazy about you. Just think about it, okay, honey?"

Piper nodded and wiped away the moisture on her face. "Thank you, Miss Cecile. I will think about it."

"Good." Cecile pulled her hand from Piper's and stuffed some tissues into it, using one to mop her own face. "Whoo. Alrighty then. Now where to?"

Piper thought a moment, then blushed. "Um . . . could we stop at the Best Buy? I need a new mouse and cable for my computer." Not many girls asked to visit the technology store on their girls' day out. But Piper wasn't most girls.

Miss Cecile chuckled. Then laughed. "Well, this will surely be a first, but hey, if you want. This is your day, girlfriend."

For the next half hour, Miss Cecile followed Piper around the store, curiously picking up various pieces of tech and examining them. Piper was in her element, but it was clear Cecile was not. "Girl, I hope you know what all these gizmo-thingies are, because I certainly don't." She picked up a Microsoft Virtual Reality headset. "What is this?"

Piper giggled at her companion's raised eyebrows and obvious consternation. "It's a VR—virtual reality—headset. When you put it on, it's like . . . like entering another world. We can ask to try it if you want."

Miss Cecile seemed so intrigued, Piper went and found a salesman eager to give a demo. Jason, the kind, if slightly pushy, salesman, fitted the headset on Miss Cecile's head and explained in layman's terms how it worked. When he started the demo, Miss Cecile's squeal of surprise had Piper laughing and the employee chuckling along.

"Nuh-uh! Piper, you seein' this? This is scary, girl! Whoa!" Each new scene brought another amusing exclamation from the woman until Piper's cheeks hurt from smiling so much. She didn't remember the last time her cheeks hurt from smiling.

It felt good.

Eventually, Piper convinced Miss Cecile that they'd taken up enough of the generous man's time and they checked out and left the store with Jason still chuckling as the door closed behind them.

Once back in the car, Miss Cecile asked, "You seen much of that young man who saved your life?"

Piper smiled at the drama in Cecile's voice. "Actually, I have a few times . . ." Miss Cecile sent her a glance fraught with meaning and Piper blushed in realization. "I mean, you know we were friends before now, right? He was my brother's best friend when we lived in Chicago." Mentioning her brother didn't bring the pang it usually did when she so much as thought of him. Strange.

"Ah," was Miss Cecile's only reply. Piper wasn't even going to try to interpret that. "You know what I think, Piper?"

"Hm?" She didn't know and wasn't sure she wanted to. But she'd quickly learned that Cecile Tompkins spoke her mind whether asked or not.

"I think the Lord brought Ezra to save your life for a reason. And I don't think either of them would appreciate you wasting it away after the trouble they went through."

Leave it to Miss Cecile to put it that way.

Piper just made a noncommittal sound and silence reigned for the rest of the drive home. She stared out the window at the passing snow-covered pine trees, lost in her thoughts. Miss Cecile's words circled through her mind. Was she wasting her life? If she thought about it, she didn't see much purpose in the empty, lonely way she was living now. Maybe God did save her life for a reason. Maybe He wanted to get her attention. He sure had a funny way of doing so if that was the case.

She bit her lip. She was tired of the pain and shame weighing down her heart. If what Miss Cecile said was true about nothing she could do ever changing God's love, then that meant . . . God loved her right now. God had loved her even when she hadn't been very complimentary towards him. It meant He had been loving her all along and was right now doing so.

All at once, a wave of something washed over her. She felt like she was drowning in it. But the good kind of drowning, like you never wanted to leave it, would never have enough of it. And then it hit her what the something was. It was love. And she realized it had been there all along, she was just too embittered against it to feel it. But now she did, and it was so strong, so warm. She felt as if it would uphold her forever. She could never drown in this sea of love; rather, she felt buoyed by it. It washed gently over her and propped her up. A single tear meandered down her face. Miss Cecile pulled into Piper's drive and as soon as she'd put the gear into park, Piper turned towards her.

"Miss Cecile, would . . . would you pray with me?"

A slow, gentle smile slid over the kind-hearted woman's face. "Honeygirl, I thought you'd never ask." She clasped Piper's hands over the gear shift, took a deep breath, and, bowing her head, offered a simple, fervent prayer. When she finished, Piper added her own words.

"Dear Lord . . . Father, thank You for loving me—for always loving me. Thank You for making that clear through Miss Cecile and Ezra. I'm sorry for hardening my heart and not listening. I'm sorry for ignoring You and blaming You. Just, thank You . . ."

Miss Cecile added a fervent amen and they both looked up at each other. Tears had streaked through Cecile's mascara and left dark tracks, and Piper was sure she looked the same.

"Girl, I've been waiting for that moment. God told me to take you shopping today. I didn't know why, but I guess we both do now." She grinned and Piper grinned back. "How do you feel?"

Piper thought for a moment and examined her heart, finding it empty of the deep pain and guilt, and full of God's love and peace and forgiveness. She now knew without a doubt God didn't hold Paul's death against her, and she knew Paul didn't either. I love you, Paul. "I feel . . . happy." She grinned. "Free. Light. Like I could squeal and dance." She giggled. "And I'm not the squealing and dancing type."

Miss Cecile hooted and pulled her in for a tight hug. "Hon, you have my permission to do all the squealin' and dancin' you want. The Lord says to dance before Him in joy."

Piper smiled at her. "Maybe I will." She was still for a moment, searching the kind brown eyes. Then she leaned in and pressed a kiss to the round, dark cheek. "Thank you, Miss Cecile."

She tsked. "La, I didn't do nothin'. Thank the Lord. Now let's get your things inside."

Once they'd unloaded the car and Miss Cecile had left, Piper stood in the dining room. She felt so full she could burst. Thank You, Jesus. Thank You! She felt like shouting from the rooftops. Then a thought hit her.

She needed to call Ezra.

Live Without You

zra groaned and pried his eyes open, rolling over. What he first thought was his alarm turned out to be the incessant ringing of his phone. It was just after 4:00 p.m. Who would be calling who didn't know he slept afternoons and worked nights? Unless it was an emergency. *Dad.* His heart leapt into his throat and he scrambled for the phone, knocking it off the nightstand in his rush. On his knees, he dug it out from under his bed and pressed it to his ear.

"Hello?" His voice was both breathless and groggy sounding.

There was a pause, then a tentative voice asked, "Ezra?"

He pulled the phone away from his ear and checked the caller ID. "Oh! Piper, are you okay? What's wrong?"

"Nothing's wrong! I'm fine. Did I wake you? I'm so sorry! I forgot you slept afternoons. I'm sorry!" Her voice sounded different . . . lighter. And apologetic.

His heart slowly settled back into its proper place. "No, no, you're fine. Just took a couple years off my life, but I'll be fine. What's up?"

"Well . . . I just thought you'd want to know."

"Know what?" *Spit it out, woman.* He normally wasn't so impatient, but when his sleep was interrupted . . . Ezra reined himself in.

"I . . . Miss Cecile prayed with me today . . ." Her voice was shy, quiet, but held a note of joy.

He stilled, heartbeat slowing as the full realization of what she'd said washed over him. "Piper . . . I don't know what to say. That's great!" He found himself grinning like a fool over her news. "Welcome to the family, sister!"

She giggled. "Thanks, Ez. It feels . . . good. I just wish I . . . hadn't wasted so much time, you know?"

Ezra nodded before realizing she couldn't see him. "I know. But word to the wise—don't waste your time thinking about the time you wasted. You'll never get anywhere doing that. Just focus on the now. Believe me, I've been there too." He had to cough to clear the huskiness from his throat.

"I'll remember that." She seemed to be thinking for a moment then continued. "When did you know, Ez? That He loved you."

He didn't have to ask who she was talking about. He thought about her question for a moment, thinking back to those days that were a testament of God's saving grace, if nothing else. He thought about how his dad had been there for him, loving him, encouraging him. And that was when he knew. He had to clear his throat again. "My dad. On my darkest days, he demonstrated to me what true love is. It doesn't leave when the going gets tough, it doesn't judge, it's patient. That was my dad. And I realized if a fallible human being could love me that way, how much more could a perfect God?"

There was a beat of silence, then, "I miss your dad." He could hear the smile in her voice and knew she was sincere.

"Hey, how about you come to church with us on Sunday? Then we can do dinner at my dad's house afterwards. Maybe Ty will join us."

Piper's hesitant chuckle came over the line. "Did you just invite a party to your dad's house without his knowledge?"

Ezra laughed. "Only because he has the bigger kitchen. But I'll be sure to ask him. What'd'ya say?"

"I don't know, Ez . . ." It still made him smile when she called him Ez. Most people did, but it seemed different coming from her.

"It's just a small church, Piper. Maybe thirty people. It actually meets in one of the houses. It's very low-key, no pressure. I wouldn't just drop you in the middle of a giant corporate worship service, I promise."

Another chuckle, and he could tell he was winning her over.

"Thanks for that," she said.

"So what do you say?"

A sigh. Then muted, "What do you say, Finley?"

He bit his cheek in amusement.

"All right, fine, but you better be serving Italian for dinner."

Ezra couldn't help but laugh. "Oh, Piper. You've got a deal. I'll pick you up?"

"Sure. I get the stitches out tomorrow, but I still don't want to drive yet."

"Alrighty, see ya then."

Ezra hung up and set the phone on his nightstand, sitting on the edge of his bed and running his fingers through his already-tousled hair. And he knew he had to admit it to himself. He kinda sorta did like Piper Redding. And not in the previous "as Paul Redding's little sister" kind of way.

Ezra pulled into the church drive—which happened to be a dirt road leading up to a large white farmhouse.

"So this is church, eh?" Piper asked.

He pulled the keys out of the ignition and flicked her an amused glance. "No one ever said church had to be in a building with a steeple and a full choir. It's really just a gathering of believers. Doesn't matter where they gather."

"Huh. Who knew?" Piper digested that somewhat surprising information.

Ezra chuckled. "I'll admit, it's not a common thought process in corporate America."

Piper started to open her door, but Ezra stopped her with a hand on her arm. "Wait for me. The ground's often slippery and we don't need you falling . . . again."

Piper glanced at him and considered sticking her tongue out, but decided against it. "It was one time, Ez. One time."

He just grinned over his shoulder at her as he climbed out and walked around to her side. He pulled the door open and helped her out, tucking her hand in his arm to escort her up the drive. He was right—it was slick. The melt from the previous day had frozen overnight, layering ice on top of snow and creating a treacherously gorgeous landscape. Fifteen or so cars already lined the driveway, leading up to the stately looking house with sparkling Christmas lights still lining the eaves and columns.

Halfway to the door, Ezra slipped, nearly falling, but righted himself in time. Piper tried to smother a laugh but didn't succeed fully. "Ah, so—"

"Don't say it," he warned, and she just chuckled and shook her head.

"You're impossible."

"So they say." But he grinned as if she'd just complimented him . . . had she just complimented him?

They made it into the house and he introduced her to their host and hostess. Ezra was guiding her to a row of chairs when she spotted a tall man, black hair sprinkled with just enough gray to make him look distinguished and the same chiseled face as Ezra coming towards them. He and Ezra exchanged a brief man-hug, then Ezra turned to her.

"Dad, you remember Piper Redding?"

"Of course! It's good to see you again, Piper." His voice was rich and deep, just how she remembered it.

She smiled and offered her hand, which he shook before pulling her into a gentle hug, surprising her. When the Bryants moved away, she'd missed this sweet man and his kind fatherliness towards her. Despite not having a huge amount of contact with him, Tom Bryant had been more of a father to her than her own dad.

They exchanged how-are-yous before Mr. Bryant led them to a group of chairs and she took a seat between the two men just as the music started playing. The first song was one that talked about the "overwhelming, never ending, reckless love of God." Piper wasn't sure whether to laugh or cry at the irony. Since it was church, she decided not to laugh, but considering she was in a public place, she decided not to cry either. As the song continued in a similar manner, she swallowed repeatedly against the emotion rising in her throat and burning in her eyes.

That God could love her so much . . . it didn't make sense, but perhaps that was the beauty of it. That He loved her so much that He'd send His Son to die in her place . . . that His Son would be willing to die in her place . . . She'd never experienced such a sacrificial love before. As the song said, it was overwhelming. It again washed over her in new waves today, reaching ever further into the darkest corners of her heart, showing her she didn't have to be afraid of losing that love, or losing those she loved.

Ezra's hand reached over and grabbed hers, giving it a light squeeze. She glanced up at him and he sent her a quick smile, understanding in his sage-colored eyes. He must have noticed her emotion, though she'd tried to hide it. His grip on her hand steadied her, reassured her. She gave it a squeeze back and turned her attention to the service.

Afterwards, the three of them made their way to Mr. Bryant's house, where Tyler met them. Ezra and Tyler insisted on making dinner, doing so with much clanging of dishes and loud peals of laughter. Mr. Bryant made coffee and engaged Piper in a conversation about her work, taking genuine interest in her job.

They were interrupted by a shout from Tyler, and both went running to the kitchen. Piper reached it first and was arrested by the sight of blood dripping from Tyler's and Ezra's hands held over the sink. Her heart pounded and her mouth felt like someone had shoved cotton balls into it. She thought she might throw up, but couldn't seem to tear her gaze from the flow of blood. Her mind flashed to that Chicago alley and all she could see was the pool of blood on the pavement. Ezra glanced over his shoulder and finally caught her gaze, remorse in his face. At first she couldn't hear him over the pounding of her heart, but finally registered his words.

"Piper, go with Dad. Tyler's all right—it's just a cut." She broke from her daze and recognized Mr. Bryant's hands on her arms, gently leading her away. As they left the kitchen, she heard Tyler say something that oddly sounded like "fudgesicle" in the tone of an expletive.

Mr. Bryant led her back to her chair in the living room and handed her her cup of tea. He reclaimed his seat across from her and gave her a grin. "Never could stand the sight of blood myself." He then changed the subject so effectively that she nearly forgot the incident.

Nearly.

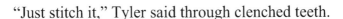

"Just stitch it," Tyler said through clenched teeth.

Ezra sluiced water over the good-sized cut on Tyler's hand again and examined it closer. "I'll do it, but are you sure you don't want an ER and an anesthetic?"

Tyler snorted, then flinched when Ezra wrapped a paper towel tightly around the wound. "Yeah, right. I'm not spending my Sunday in an ER. Just do it."

"Fine. I'll grab my kit from my car." Ezra quickly jogged out to his car. He felt terrible that Piper had seen the blood. He should have known she'd be sensitive to it. She'd gone white as a sheet and froze up. He almost thought she was going to pass out. Ezra hoped the look he'd sent his dad communicated sufficiently the need to distract her. She had been making such progress, then Tyler had to go and . . . He bit the inside of his cheek. It wasn't Tyler's fault the knife had slipped. Ezra sent up a quick prayer that the event wouldn't bring up too many traumatic memories for Piper as he hurried back to the house and set up the items he needed to stitch the gash closed.

"Flaming jack-o'-lanterns, why does such a tiny cut hurt so bad?"

Ezra bit back a chuckle. Leave it to Tyler to come up with such a . . . colorful expression. "Aw, buck up, baby. Like you said, it's tiny." Tyler just glared and gnawed on his lip as Ezra pulled the needle through his skin. After being accused of being a wimp, nothing would stop Tyler from proving otherwise. He was anything but wimpy, but it did shut him up.

Six stitches and a gauze wrap later, he was good to go, although grumbling. Ezra quickly poked his head in the living room and found Piper listening intently to a story his father was telling. The color had come back in her face and she looked at ease, despite the few lines around her mouth indicating a stress headache, he guessed. He hurried back into the kitchen and finished preparing the meal, Ty helping as best as possible one-handedly.

After his dad said the blessing, they dug into the cream sauce and chicken pasta, salad, and garlic bread. He noticed Piper sending worried glances Tyler's way for the first few minutes before asking, "Is your hand okay, Tyler?"

Tyler held up his hand and examined it. "What, this? Pssh. It was nothing—didn't even hurt," he said nonchalantly.

Ezra snorted into his water glass, but didn't bother calling him out on his bluff for Piper's sake. She looked relieved to hear it was nothing.

11

The sky was inky and the street lamps reflected yellow light off the thick layer of snow that covered everything. Ezra pulled into Piper's driveway and, as he put the vehicle in park, she turned towards him, the streetlight softly illuminating the lines of his face.

She fiddled with her hands for a moment before looking up at him. "Ez, I'm sorry for . . . for earlier." She squirmed and felt her cheeks redden at the memory. "I don't know . . . I saw the blood, and I couldn't . . ." Fumbling awkwardly to a stop, she glanced down at her lap.

Ezra placed his hand over her fidgeting ones. "It's okay, Piper. I get it." His smile gently crinkled the corners of his eyes and she found herself smiling back.

"Thanks," she whispered.

He turned to climb out of the car, but then stopped. "Oh! Wait." Reaching back behind their seats, he rummaged in the back before facing her again and placing a small box wrapped in pretty blue tissue paper in her lap. "I have something for you."

"Ez . . ." She gave him a look and he just grinned.

"Open it."

She gently tore the wrapping away and lifted the lid on the small shoebox. Inside was a worn, masculine-looking leather Bible that looked slightly familiar. She lifted it out and ran her fingers over the smooth, soft leather before sending Ezra another questioning glance.

"Look inside," was he all he said.

She thumbed through the pages, finding many of them marked with pencil underlinings and notes in the margin in a handwriting that also looked familiar . . . almost like . . . She inhaled and met Ezra's eyes. He nodded, a soft look on his face. Piper turned to the flyleaf and read the inscription.

"Paul Aaron Redding."

Tears cascaded down her face but she barely noticed them. Paul's Bible. She was holding Paul's Bible. She never knew a single object could mean so much. She read the words printed beneath the first line in the careful, precise manner so characteristic of her brother.

"To my friend and comrade, Ezra Bryant. May you find in this what you are looking for."

"No, Ezra, no. I can't take this!" She tried to shove it back into his hands, tears still streaming. He only wrapped his hands around hers holding the Bible and pressed firmly.

"You're not taking it—I'm giving it. And I think . . . I think Paul would have wanted you to have it. I wore it out pretty good," he smiled ruefully. "And I know you will too. Take good care of it, Piper." He placed the Bible back in her lap and handed her a tissue.

She mopped her face. "Thank you. I don't know what else to say." It felt so insufficient, like an understatement. But it was all she knew to say.

"Well." He rubbed his jaw. "Can I at least give you an awkward hug?"

Piper giggled. "Of course." She put her arm around his neck and he wrapped his arms around her in what was indeed an awkward hug over the gear shift. But it felt perfect, somehow.

Later, Piper crawled into bed and pulled up the fuzzy blanket, Finley curling up at her feet. She pulled Paul's Bible into her lap and flipped it open to the frontispiece, rereading the inscription, running her fingers over her brother's familiar script. She flipped the page over, and noticed another inscription in a different hand—bold, blocky, steady. "To Piper Redding, a friend and sister in the Lord. If you ever doubt God's love, read Psalm 18. He loves you and He's fighting for you. And He won't stop. —Ezra C. Bryant."

Piper pulled her knees up to her chest and rested her forehead on them, hugging the book to her chest, letting the tears flow. Would they ever stop? At least these ones were born of love instead of pain, peace instead of guilt.

Three weeks flew by in a rush. Piper and Ezra had regular phone and text conversations, many of them instigated by Piper asking questions about certain verses in the Bible or other things about her newfound faith. Ezra was slightly surprised that she chose him to answer her questions. And he couldn't help but feel these types of conversations would lead to a more specific sort of relationship in the future. But he didn't want to push things for her. He knew she was still adjusting to moving to a new state, new faith, and finally recovering from the emotional trauma of the previous several years. So he bided his time.

One afternoon he got a text that simply read: "How can He love me if I've messed up so much?"

Ezra sighed. It wasn't the first time she'd asked this question, although it was worded differently each time.

He started to type out a response, but then backspaced. It would be easier to call. He'd always been better with verbal communications than putting words on paper—or in text, in this case. As the call rang, he sent up a quick prayer. "Give me your words, Lord."

She answered and it sounded like her voice quavered slightly.

He cut to the chase. "Have you read First John yet?"

The sound of pages flipping met his ear. She must have her phone on speaker. "Um . . . I don't think so."

"Well, First John talks a lot about love. It mentions more than once the phrase, 'God is love.' Love is in His being, Piper. It's who He is. There's no way He cannot love someone. It's like . . . you're left-handed, right? You were born that way. You'll always be left-handed. It's in your DNA."

There was silence for a moment. "I actually tried to teach myself to be right-handed when I was a freshman."

He chuckled. "Okay, so maybe not the most flawless comparison, but you get the idea, right? No matter what one does, it can't change who He is. He is love."

There was silence and he wondered if they'd lost the connection. "Piper?"

Her voice was soft and he pressed the phone tighter to his ear in an attempt to hear her. "Even if I killed someone?"

Ezra sat back in his chair. Whoa, not expecting that one.

"What . . . what do you mean, Piper?" What was she talking about?

"That bullet was meant for me. I should have died." She was crying now, the weight of grief and shame heavy in her voice.

His heart hurt for her and he bit his lip. He thought she was past this. Why was it coming back now? "You mean at the skating rink?"

"No. Chicago, Ez." Her tone pleaded with him to understand. "I was there. Paul heard the shooting and shoved me out of the way. He died because of me. It's my fault. I killed him."

The information settled on his chest like a two-ton brick. She had been there. She had been with Paul. He closed his eyes and rested his forehead on his fist. Oh good Lord . . . He couldn't imagine. That particular bit of information was not in the news article. The sound of Piper's crying was still coming over the phone. He gentled his voice. "Hey, Piper, shh. It's not your fault. You know Paul would have protected others before himself anyway, whether it was his sister or someone else. It's who he was." The past tense still burned in his throat. "He was a rescuer. That's why he became a paramedic. If he had to do it over again, do you think he would have done it differently? If you had to do it over again, was there anything you could have done differently?"

She sniffled.

"Is there, Piper? Is there anything you could have done differently?" His voice was gentle, but firm, commanding an answer.

"No," she hiccupped.

"No, there's not. Piper, you can't take this on. Things happen. And that's all there is to it. You can't move on until you let the guilt go. When my mom died . . . You know, Piper. You know. I blamed myself. It ate me up until I wanted to give up. But as soon as I accepted the fact—the truth—that it wasn't my fault, I was free. God didn't hold it against me. My dad didn't. And I needed to not hold it against myself. Okay?"

Ezra could almost see her nodding. "Okay." She took a deep breath. "I thought I was past this . . . but I had another dream last night, and just . . . just couldn't shake it off. I tried reading my Bible, but Leviticus wasn't helping much," she said ruefully.

Ezra chuckled. "Yeah, I can see that. Hey, you sound tired. Why don't you rest for a bit, and I'll bring over pizza in a couple hours for an early dinner. All right?"

"I'm scared to sleep," she admitted softly.

He tsked sympathetically. "Listen, whenever you have another nightmare, call me. Anytime. I may not answer if I happen to be on a call, but I'll try."

"Ez . . ." she started to protest, but he cut her off.

"You don't have to be alone anymore, Piper. God's there, and I'm here. You're my friend, and I want to help you." And be more than that, he mentally added.

"Fine." She finally agreed, more life coming back into her tone. "But I'm at least paying for the pizza."

Yes! There was the sass . . . He laughed. "The gentleman in me protests, but if it helps you sleep at night, you may," he said, then winced at his unfortunate turn of phrase.

"I feel like I keep saying this, but thank you, Ezra. I've never had a friend quite like you before . . ." She added the last sentence in a soft voice.

Did that work in his favor? He hoped so . . . "Then just stop thanking me," he said, a smile spreading across his face. "Go sleep now, and I'll see you later."

"All right. Bye, Ez."

Ezra ended the call and stared at the phone in his hand. Then he pressed speed dial.

"Dad, we've got a problem. I think I'm falling in love . . ."

A loud laugh and hearty "About time!" was the response.

After she hung up, Piper made herself a soothing cup of hot cocoa and curled up on the couch with Paul's Bible. She turned the pages until she found the book of First John and started reading the first chapter. As she read, she took note of the many underlined verses and notes in the margin written in her brother's oh-so-familiar, precise hand. The first two verses of chapter two were underlined and she read the note next to them. *"What a blessing that we have an advocate with God! He cleansed and continues to cleanse us from our sins, so we can always have access to the pure and holy Father."*

Piper smiled as the note jogged a memory of Paul and Ezra discussing this same topic. She'd overheard part of their conversation from the other room and had stepped into the kitchen to hear the rest. Paul was gesticulating with soapsuds-covered hands and his face was alive and alight with a passion that had taken her aback at first. Paul was a laid-back kind of guy, but when he cared deeply about something, his passion was quite clear. He'd only ever been that passionate about his faith, his job as a paramedic—being a rescuer, as Ezra had said—and . . . her. He'd been her advocate, for as long as she could remember. For forever. From scraped knees when she was little to bullies in high school, he'd been there, protecting her, defending her, loving her, encouraging her. A single tear dropped on the page and she quickly blotted it away before it could damage the paper. Now that she wasn't spending so much time angry at the world, she had time to miss Paul. Years could only dull the ache in her heart.

She read until she reached the end of the book, then kept reading. Her eyelids started to droop and she rested her head against the couch and quickly dropped into the sleep of the dreamless.

Piper startled awake a short time later to the shrill ringing of her phone, and bolted upright. She rubbed the sleep from her eyes and brushed the hair back from her face as she answered the phone. "Hello?"

"I'm on your porch." It was Ezra.

"Oh! Sorry, one sec." She dropped the phone onto the couch and crossed the room to open the door. "Sorry again. I was sleeping."

He smiled. "I figured."

She led the way into the kitchen and pulled paper plates from the cabinet. "How much do I owe you for the pizza? Thanks for bringing it."

Ezra didn't answer, and she scowled. "Ezra, I am paying for the pizza."

Ezra sighed, chuckled, and shook his head. "Fine. If you insist."

"I do."

He shrugged and handed over the receipt before sitting down.

"So I read First John." Piper said between mouthfuls of cheesy goodness.

Ezra swallowed his own mouthful. "Go on—admit that I was right."

Piper rolled her eyes. "Tyler was right—you are bossy, and arrogant too," she said playfully.

He just smirked and took another bite of pizza. "I'll let you get away with saying that only because I like you—and my mom told me not to fight girls."

Piper inwardly froze but tried to keep a nonchalant facade in place. He liked her? What did that mean? She was probably reading more into that than he'd meant. She took another bite of pizza and listened and laughed as Ezra launched into a story about his punishment the time he took a toy from a girl at the playground.

Piper suddenly gasped and launched out of her chair, causing Ezra to startle and jump up as well. "What? What's wrong?"

"What time is it?" As she asked the question, she pulled her phone out of her pocket. "Almost 4:30. Drat. I promised a client I'd have their project done by five tonight. Do you mind? It won't take me long."

He shrugged and spread his hands. "Hey, you gotta do what ya gotta do. Go ahead. I'll put these things away." He gestured to their dishes on the table.

What a sweetheart. "You're such a dear, I could—" She suddenly broke off, blushing furiously. Had she really almost said she could kiss him? A peck-on-the-cheek kiss, of course, not a kiss kiss. "—I could feed you ice cream. There's some in the freezer," she finished lamely. He chuckled and she blushed again, hurrying to her desk as he grabbed the dishes off the table and carried them into the kitchen.

What an idiot she was.

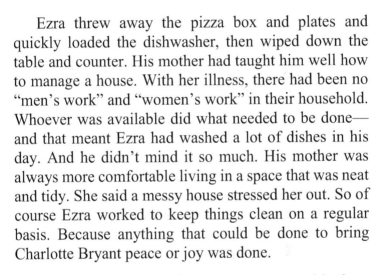

Ezra threw away the pizza box and plates and quickly loaded the dishwasher, then wiped down the table and counter. His mother had taught him well how to manage a house. With her illness, there had been no "men's work" and "women's work" in their household. Whoever was available did what needed to be done— and that meant Ezra had washed a lot of dishes in his day. And he didn't mind it so much. His mother was always more comfortable living in a space that was neat and tidy. She said a messy house stressed her out. So of course Ezra worked to keep things clean on a regular basis. Because anything that could be done to bring Charlotte Bryant peace or joy was done.

Ezra sighed and scrubbed a hand across his face, wishing he could scrub away the grief as easily. Nine years could never erase the pain of watching one's mother die, day by day, month by month, year by year. He squeezed his eyes shut for a brief moment against the memories that assailed. He wasn't going there . . . not today.

Looking around Piper's home, it was clear she didn't feel the same way about her surroundings as his mother had. It amused him. Somehow the mess around him was so uniquely Piper he couldn't help but find it adorable. Books littered the end tables and floor by the couch, as did a few pillows. Her corner desk looked like a technology store had thrown up over it, and he didn't know what half the gadgets were. A glance to his left showed a room with an unmade bed and articles of clothing tossed haphazardly across the blue sheets. Certainly not as unkempt as Tyler's apartment, but chaotic nonetheless. It would take a lot to rival Tyler's housekeeping skills . . . or lack thereof, rather.

Ezra wandered over to stand behind where Piper sat at her corner desk, fully engrossed in her work. The computer showed a black screen with a jumble of tiny characters spread across it. Piper was typing rapidly, adding more gibberish to the already incomprehensible mess on the screen. What was she doing? He asked, and at the sound of his voice, she jumped. "Oh! Forgot you were there."

Ezra chuckled. Even when she was younger, she'd become so engrossed in her books or schoolwork it would take several attempts to get her attention. He tried to focus on what she was saying.

"This—" She gestured to the screen, "is a text editor. All these characters are behind every page on the web. It's a markup language called HTML—HyperText Markup Language. Many people confuse it with programming languages like Java and C++, but it's really different. See, these are each considered HTML elements and there's the content you see—" she looked up at his face and must have read the confusion written there, as she then abbreviated her explanation. "Look." Switching windows, she pulled up a website for an accounting firm. "All you see in the text editor is what is working behind the scenes to create this website. Make sense?"

He slowly shook his head, bewildered. "No. But I'll take your word for it."

She huffed a laugh and pulled up the foreign-looking document again, hunching towards the screen. "I'll be done in a just a minute. When do you have to get to work?"

"I don't. Got a day off today. I was hoping you'd take a walk with me. It's cold, but sunny out, and you need some sunshine. You're pale as a ghost."

"Mm . . ." She just absently rubbed her cheek, absorbed in her work once again. He shook his head and pulled his phone out, scrolling through emails until she finished.

Ten minutes later, she spun in her office chair to face him. "There. I'm done. Sorry about that. What did you want to do?"

Ezra pocketed his phone. "I thought we'd take a walk."

She glanced out the window and grimaced. "It's freezing."

He laughed. "Welcome to Washington, darling. Go get your coat. Doctor's orders."

She grumbled as she went to grab her coat, muttering under her breath. "You are bossy, just like Paul."

Ezra had to swallow at the sudden emotion rising in his throat. That was one of the greatest compliments she could give him.

FOUR WEEKS LATER . . .

oday was the day. The sun was shining. And Ezra Bryant was freaking out. He smoothed a hand over his hair for the fifth time and exhaled, square jaw and green eyes reflecting back at him in the bathroom mirror. *Let's do this, man,* he mentally coached himself.

He was finally making the leap. He only hoped Piper didn't run screaming.

Piper checked her reflection in the rearview mirror and smoothed a hand across her hair before stepping out of her car into the brisk, early March air. A good portion of the snow had melted already, leaving large brown and green patches. Another heavy load of the white crystallized liquid and more freezing temps were forecasted for the next week, but she'd enjoy the slight warmth while she could. She'd jumped at the opportunity to take a walk in the park with Ezra after church when he'd asked her. His voice had seemed a little odd when he made the request . . . Despite what he teased, she wasn't a hermit. She just didn't find the same pleasure in slowly freezing like he did. She smiled and shook her head, then caught sight of Ezra across the street. He looked both ways before crossing to her. Was it just her or did his face light up when he saw her?

"Hey."

"Hey . . . Uh." He coughed. "Thanks for meeting me."

"Of course. It's a gorgeous day for a walk." She tilted her head up towards the sunlight that filtered through the trees as they set off on one of the paths through the park. Ezra was strangely silent.

"So . . . what did you think of Robert's sermon this morning?" The message had been based on Acts chapter two. Piper had found those verses strange and far-fetched sounding, but Robert, one of the leaders of the small home church, had expounded upon and explained them in a new way that made more sense. She'd found it very interesting and apparently so did Ezra, as that finally got him talking.

They discussed it at length as they continued down the pathway. They had moved on to a different topic by the time they reached a small, tucked-away coffee shop. He offered to get them a drink and Piper waited off to the side while he ordered. A sparrow sang from the treetops and two mourning doves flitted on the fence. Her first winter in Washington was turning out to be quite beautiful and so peaceful. Chicago was nothing compared to small-town Washington.

Ezra handed her her drink and they stepped back outside. She thanked him with a smile and took a sip, grateful to have something warm to drink. She nearly choked on the first sip of the hot, bitter brew. She managed to swallow before coughing, her eyes watering. Her tongue was convinced it had just tasted sludge.

Ezra took the cup back from her as she caught her breath and looked concerned. "Too hot? I'm sorry." His voice was remorseful.

Piper shook her head and winced. "What did you order?"

"A simple hot cocoa! I promise." He muttered something about fancy coffee shops as he squinted at the markings on the side of the cup. "Oh. Oops. I gave you my coffee. This one must be yours." He held up the other cup with a sheepish grin. "Sorry."

Piper chuckled at the look on his face. Then couldn't help laughing. He joined in and they laughed so hard she collapsed onto a nearby bench, leaning forward and clutching her stomach. They finally recovered themselves and Ezra handed her the correct cup this time. She gave him a wary glance before checking the contents herself, which set him off again.

It felt so right. Laughing. Drinking hot cocoa. With Ezra. It almost scared her how natural it felt.

They finally set off down the path again, sipping their respective drinks in a peaceful silence. Finally, Ezra spoke. "Piper, I have something to say to you," he said in a rush.

She grinned up at him. He was just shy of a head taller than her. "Those sound like fighting words, Ezra Bryant."

He chuckled, but sounded nervous. "They're not. I . . ." He stopped walking, looking down at his feet before meeting her gaze. "I like spending time with you, Piper."

Her breath caught and she didn't quite know what to say. She bit her lip. "I . . . like spending time with you too . . ." Where on earth was this heading?

Ezra continued walking, his gaze focused on the distant Cascade Mountains. "I've been doing a lot of thinking, and praying, of course, and talking to my dad. And . . . I was wondering . . . if you would be interested in . . . pursuing a different sort of relationship with me. A . . . courtship, of sorts."

Whoa. He was asking . . . Piper's heart rate picked up and her palms grew sweaty against the sides of the styrofoam cup she held. Ezra must have noted the alarm spreading across her face because he held up a hand and quickly continued. "I'm making a muddle of this . . . argh." He rubbed the back of his neck. "I like you, Piper. You're smart, wise, funny, tenderhearted. I've seen you searching after God voraciously these past several weeks. Your dedication to your work and to learning more about your faith inspires me. I want to see if . . . if we could be something more . . ."

Piper didn't even know what to think at first. But as he talked, an apprehension welled up in her that she couldn't quite put her finger on. The thought of such a committed relationship . . . it terrified her.

"Ez . . . I don't . . . I . . . I need—" She stumbled over her words, growing increasingly agitated as she tried to articulate . . . what, she didn't know.

Ezra instantly stepped into caregiver mode, placing a comforting hand on her shoulder and shushing her. "Hey, it's okay. You don't have to say anything right now. Just think on it, okay?"

"I'm sorry . . . I . . ." She felt shaken. She needed to think. To be alone.

"It's okay, it's okay. You don't have to be sorry for anything."

She nodded. "I should . . . get home now." She said, not meeting his eyes. She'd probably break down if she saw his face. She felt bad for leaving him this way, but . . . she just couldn't.

He nodded gently. "We'll talk later. Drive safe."

Piper turned and walked back across the park to her car.

The fear had come back. And she hated herself for letting it.

Ezra watched Piper as she trudged back along the path, feeling like he'd failed somehow yet again. Maybe it was too soon. But he thought the timing was right. He couldn't forget the look of alarm that had spread across her face as he spoke. And he hated that he had caused it.

"God, what did I do wrong?" His groan scattered a few birds on the ground a few yards away. Piper's car pulled away from the curb and he turned and set off at a jog through the park.

Ezra finally reached the edge of the park and pulled out his phone, winded from his run. He pressed the speed dial.

"Dad, how many times did Mom say no before she said yes?"

His father's answer was prompt, needing no preamble or explanation. "Six."

Ezra sighed and a light, sympathetic chuckle came through the line. "Hang in there—just give her some space."

He sighed again.

Live Without You

Piper curled up on the couch, frustrated with herself and the world. It'd been two days since Ezra had asked her and she'd run away like Finley when the phone rang.

"God, why? Why do I feel this way?" she asked aloud.

Finley poked her head out from under the chair where she'd been napping, clearly confusing Piper's prayer with the call for food. Piper ignored her.

The word came softly like a gently spoken whisper. *Trust.*

That was the problem. She hadn't realized until now how much she'd come to trust Ezra . . . and it scared her. By trusting him, she gave him ways to hurt her. It was why she'd decided love wasn't worth the risk. He could leave. He could die. And she'd been there, done that.

It hurt. Too much.

If you knew your brother would die, would you have chosen to not have a brother at all?

The thought came out of nowhere and struck her like a physical blow. Would she have? She searched her heart and the answer she found there was emphatic.

No.

Love was worth the risk. She thought about how grieved God must have been by her anger and accusations. Yet He still chose to love her anyway. True love endured. It overcame fear. She scrambled for her Bible, turning to First John. "Perfect love casts out fear." Would she give it up to avoid the potential pain?

No.

"God?" she whispered.

His answer soothed her soul and brought instant peace to her mind.

She reached for her phone. It rang and rang. And rang . . . Finally going to voicemail. She huffed and hung up, waiting a few seconds before trying again. And again.

The shrill ringing startled him from his thoughts and the head of lettuce he'd been chopping for his dinner rolled to the floor. Ezra growled and picked it up before reaching for his phone. He jabbed the answer button. "Hello?" He winced. His voice sounded terse and short, making his greeting almost menacing.

"First John 4:18, Ez." It was Piper's voice, sounding breathless.

"I'm sorry?" He rubbed his forehead, confused.

"First John 4:18," she repeated. "Do you know it?"

He wasn't sure she'd ever sounded this excited. He was going to take that as a good sign. "Um . . . refresh my memory."

"'There is no fear in love, but perfect love casts out fear,'" she recited. "I'm not going to lie, you terrified me, Ezra Bryant." He tensed as she continued. "But do you know what God asked me?"

She seemed to be waiting for an answer. "No. What?"

"He asked if I had the choice to not know, not love Paul, would I have taken it? Even if I knew he was going to leave me?" Her voice choked and his heart clenched. Maybe she wasn't ready for this. . . .

"Would you have taken that choice with your mother?" she asked.

Ouch. He didn't have to think about it. "No," he said softly. Because while those days were the most tortuous days he'd ever experienced, he wouldn't trade a single moment with his mother for anything else in the world.

"No. I've now learned to treasure and embrace those memories of days spent with my big brother instead of shoving them away and locking them in a box. It hurts, Ezra. And I'm not going to say it won't be hard trusting God in this. People leave, Ez. It's what my life's been full of and what I'm most scared of. From my parents' abuse, to Paul's death, even to you and your dad moving across the country. Although I didn't realize how much that hurt until recently." Her voice was soft, but then grew in intensity, showing again her adorable sassy side that reminded him so much of his mother. "But you know what? I've decided I don't want to hide away in a little house in Nowheresville, Washington, trusting no one and being alone till the day I die. So—" She paused and he gulped, pretty sure now he knew where she was going with this.

"So?"

"So, yeah, I'll be your girlfriend!" she squealed.

He let out a whoop, pumping his fist in the air. Then she was laughing too.

"You're a pretty amazing lady, Piper."

He could hear the smile in her voice. "Yeah? Well, I think you're pretty amazing too, Ezra."

"So . . ." He coughed. "How about dinner? I know I'm not going to be able to sleep this afternoon. I'll just have to drink several cups of coffee when I get to work."

She chuckled. "Why do I not believe that doesn't already happen on a regular basis?"

Live Without You

15

Piper strolled along the rutted pathway through the park, her hand tucked securely in Ezra's arm, autumn leaves crunching beneath their feet. There had been silence between them for the last several minutes, but it was the peaceful kind, a comfortableness existing between them that felt as natural as breathing. She looked back on where she'd been eight months ago and marveled at all God had worked in both their lives.

Eight months ago had found her alone in a strange place, confused, lonely, angry at the world and God, and recovering from a gunshot wound to her shoulder. Now, she felt at home in the little town of Arlington and she'd finally learned to put her trust in God and her fears behind her—although that was still an everyday process. And she had a friend . . . one she hoped to marry one day.

She snuck a glance up at him. Dark brown hair was unruly and long, dancing in the breeze. Similarly colored stubble lined his square jaw with a five-o'clock shadow and in his eyes was the compassion and kindness that made him so good at his job. She respected him—this man who threw his all into everything he did, taking more thought for those around him than for himself. And she'd grown to love him—the man who had been there for her, watching out for her, holding her while she cried, and quoting scripture to her over the phone in the night when nightmares tormented her and fear threatened to take her heart in its icy grip again. He silently loved, laying down his life for her, always pointing her back to God first, both of them knowing that their relationship was a trio, not a duo.

"Piper . . ."

"Hm?" She looked up at him again. He heaved a deep breath and she frowned. "What is it? Is something wrong?"

"No, no, sorry. I . . ." He looked around as if expecting someone else to be there. She followed his gaze but he grabbed her arms and swung her back around to face him. "I've been doing some thinking."

She chuckled. "When are you not, Ez? Your brain's always swirling. Makes me dizzy."

He grinned down at her. She could live with seeing that look on his face every day for the rest of her life.

"Well, I think you'll like what I've been thinking about this time." He fished in his back pocket as if searching for his wallet.

"Don't tell me you lost your wallet . . . again." He'd lost his wallet a few weeks ago, but lucky for him, Tyler had found it on a sidewalk outside a home where they'd responded to a call.

"Nope, still there." He grinned again, looking almost . . . giddy. Something was up. Ezra Bryant didn't do giddy.

He suddenly looked off into the left middle-distance. "What is that?" he asked.

She looked, but didn't see anything out of the ordinary. "I don't know what you're talking . . . about." She looked back at him and her sentence faltered. He'd dropped to a knee in front of her. She lowered a brow and took a step back. "Ez . . . ?"

He took a breath as if his life depended on it, then let it out, a serious look now on his face. "Piper Marie Redding, we've known each other for a long time."

She put a hand over her mouth and took another step back. He wasn't . . .

"These last several months of getting to know you more, I've decided that I don't want to have to live without you. We've both strived to seek God first in our relationship and I feel like He's calling us to the next step." He sucked in another breath and she clenched both her hands over her mouth, tears slowly streaming down her face.

"I love you, Piper, with all that's in me, and would be honored to call you my wife. Will you marry me?" He held up a simple gold band with a modestly sized diamond in the middle, circled by tiny amethysts. She didn't know what to say . . . she was still too shocked. She always thought she'd see it coming, but he'd completely surprised her.

"Piper," he groaned. "This isn't helping my ego!"

A giggle burst forth. "Yes! A thousand yeses!"

"One will cut it." He grinned, standing up. She threw her arms around his neck and he wrapped his arms around her, spinning in a slow circle. She pulled back and looked up into his face, meeting his green eyes that sparkled with unshed tears.

"I love you, Ezra Bryant."

He cupped her face in his gentle hands and pressed a kiss to her forehead. "Not as much as I love you," he whispered. Taking her left hand, he slid the ring onto her fourth finger. It fit perfectly. Maybe that was why Miss Cecile had taken a sudden interested in her jewelry collection just last week.

He held up her hand and turned around. "Smile for the camera!"

"Wha—?" Tyler and Mr. Bryant had appeared from the trees, grinning and giving them thumbs-up as Tyler snapped pictures left and right.

Piper just laughed and shook her head. Hugs and congratulations were exchanged all around. Tyler, when finally finished snapping pictures, gave her a bro hug and a fist bump. And Mr. Bryant gave her a tight, gentle hug, then pulled back and cupped her chin in his giant hand. "Welcome to the family, Piper." She smiled her thanks through glistening tears and he dropped a kiss on her hair before stepping away to give Ezra a fatherly hug and congratulations.

Laughter filled the park, and she knew she was the happiest woman in the world.

If such a thing were possible, Ezra would think he was floating on air. God was in His heaven, and Piper Redding, the love of his life, had agreed to be his wife. All was right with the world.

After his proposal, a few close friends from church joined them at the park for a celebration. He glanced over at Piper. She'd been chatting happily since they'd left ten minutes ago—a sure sign she was excited. At the rate of her words per minute currently, she was beyond excited. And that thrilled him. She'd already experienced more pain and heartache in her short twenty-seven years than most people older than his thirty years had.

He tuned back in to what Piper was saying, loving the sound of her voice and her giggle. She'd gone from saying how surprised she'd been and how happy she was to have all their close friends there, and now had stopped to take a breath and examine her ring for possibly the tenth time.

"It's so beyond perfect, Ez! I can't even tell you."

He smiled through the windshield as he spun the wheel and turned onto the four-lane divided highway leading out of town. "I'm glad. Miss Cecile, and even my dad provided their expert opinions."

She sent him a mock glare and said accusingly, "You sent Miss Cecile snooping!"

Ezra laughed heartily. She was quick. "I did not. Not really. She was just interested in seeing your jewelry box."

She raised her eyebrows. "It's called snooping, Bryant."

He laughed again and she joined in. There was quiet after that except for the muted sounds of the vehicle. Piper reached over and put her hand on top of his resting on the gear shift, squeezing lightly. "I love you, Ezra Bryant."

He opened his mouth to reply, but a large, dark shadow suddenly appeared to the left in his peripheral vision. Gripping the wheel, he swerved before a fierce jolt shook him and rattled his body head to toe. He had one thought as fiery pain exploded and the world flashed white before he spiraled uncontrollably into a dark void.

Piper.

Live Without You

16

Piper blinked slowly and pulled herself out of the blackness. Her mind registered cool air blowing across her face, tainted with the acrid scent of burnt rubber. Something dripped down her face and she saw a splotch of red. Blood. Again. She fought the nausea rising.

A soothing voice spoke to her right. "It's okay, ma'am, you're all right. Just hold still. Can you tell me your name?"

"P-Piper. Piper Redding." She turned her head towards the voice and saw a fireman cutting her loose from the car. Car. The accident. Ezra! Her brain kicked into gear all at once and panic clawed up her throat, making it hard to breathe. "Ezra! Ezra, where is he?"

"Just stay calm, ma'am," the fireman answered in that irritatingly soothing voice. "Was he the driver?"

"Yes, yes, where is he? Is he all right?" Hysteria rose in her voice and she didn't try to hide it.

No. This couldn't be happening. Not after all she'd been through.

"He's okay for now; we pulled him out before you, and they are loading him in the ambulance right now." For now. What did that mean? If he died . . . she wasn't sure she could take one more thing. *God, where are You? You said You'd be here . . . but I don't feel You right now.* "Now, please hold still. You could be injured." His voice now held a note of dismay as she tried to push past him and get out of the car. She ignored his protests and slipped out of the car, but was confronted with a paramedic and a gurney.

"I'm fine, I'm not hurt. Really, I'm fine. Please just let me go to him!" She wasn't above begging.

The paramedic spoke up this time. "You're bleeding." She gestured to Piper's cheek. "Just let me check you over real quick, then we'll take you to the hospital to check on him." Over the woman's shoulder, Piper saw other paramedics loading a stretcher into an ambulance with Ezra's still, blood-covered form on it. With a cry, she sprang past the paramedic and fireman, running towards the ambulance, one thought consuming her mind.

She couldn't lose him.

She couldn't lose him.

She couldn't lose him.

A large form stepped in front of her, and she collided into it before she reached the ambulance. It was Tyler. He wrapped his arms around her as her knees buckled and she sank to the pavement, sobs wracking her body. His soothing words couldn't penetrate the icy fear slowly gripping her heart with its cold tentacles. The ambulance peeled away, siren screaming.

She didn't know how long they knelt on the pavement, but it felt like an eternity as the fear, grief, and uncertainty of the future poured out in salty liquid. Finally, she sat back, taking a shuddering deep breath. She met Tyler's eyes and saw his own pain reflected in them. "Are you okay?" he asked.

She nodded, then shook her head. She didn't know how she felt anymore. She felt numb, and somehow, she knew that was worse than the previous raw pain she'd felt.

"How's your head?"

Piper gingerly touched a finger to a cut on her cheek. "It hurts a little, but not much."

He nodded and led her over to the back of the remaining ambulance. "Let me clean the cuts on your face, then I'll take you to the hospital, okay?"

She nodded and took a deep breath. Now that the shock and panic had worn off, she tuned in to the bone-deep ache that had spread over her entire body and the headache that intensified as Tyler shined a penlight in her eyes to check her pupils and gently prodded the bruises on her face.

"What happened?" She sent a glance over her shoulder towards Ezra's olive-colored Subaru. The entire driver's door was completely smashed in, and the whole vehicle resembled more a hunk of aluminum than a car. A large black truck sat empty not far away, the grill dented in. More tears leaked out at the sight, stinging the cuts on her cheeks. Funny how she hadn't noticed them before.

"Hey." Tyler gently turned her back towards him and started cleaning the wounds on her face. "You gotta stop crying. You know Ez hates when you do. In answer to your question, the pickup truck missed a red light and t-boned the driver's side of the car. Broken glass did this." He gestured to her face, then shook his head. "It's by God's hand alone that you're both alive."

"And Ezra?" she asked softly.

He didn't meet her eyes, busying himself with applying a butterfly bandage to one of the larger cuts. "He's probably got a few broken ribs and head trauma; some cuts and bruises. But I don't think his spine or pelvis was broken. So that's good."

"So he's going to be okay?"

Resting his hands on her shoulders, his blue eyes met her brown ones. "I can only pray so, Piper."

———————————◆———————————

Piper fiddled with her hands as she sat in the ER waiting room with Tyler. He'd made a valiant attempt to cheer her up—what he did best—but she just shook her head, and he lapsed into silence. He'd insisted on her being examined when they reached the ER, despite her protests. They wouldn't hear anything on Ezra for a while anyway he'd said, and he was right. She felt like she'd been waiting for hours when it had only been a half hour by the clock on the wall.

The kindly doctor who'd examined her had pronounced her lucky to have no other injuries than the cuts on her face and a few on her arms. She'd cheated death again, Tyler had joked. He had no idea . . . Sure, she'd cheated death again, but at what cost? The expense of someone she loved. Her faith felt shaken and her heart wounded, raw. Why was this happening to her? Again? She was trying so desperately to cling to the promises she knew, but fear invaded once again, wrapping its cold fingers around her.

Another minute ticked agonizingly by and the doors swooshed open for the hundredth time since they'd been sitting there. A tall man in business attire with dark, salt-speckled hair entered. He looked towards the information desk before catching sight of her and Tyler and walking hurriedly towards them.

Mr. Bryant.

He instantly pulled her into a tight hug that melted her fears somewhat. She choked back the tears threatening to rise again.

"I'm so glad you're okay," he said, voice choked as he released her and looked searchingly into her face, gently fingering one of the bandages there. His son had been severely wounded in a car accident and here he was worried about her? His kindness soothed over one of the scraped-raw-again scars in her heart. Keeping one arm snug around her shoulders in a comforting half hug, he turned to Tyler, who'd stood up when he entered, and raised a single brow. Ty shook his head.

"Nothing yet, but it shouldn't be long now." He checked his watch again and glanced towards the doors leading back into the ER.

Mr. Bryant seated her back in her chair and took the one next to it, loosening his tie and unbuttoning the top button of his dress shirt with a deep sigh. He'd obviously come straight from his downtown office where he'd gone after their little party. Tyler retold the story of what had happened and she was grateful she didn't have to. He had been not far behind them on his way home, and she was glad for his assistance and support as she gave her statement to the officers and navigated the maze of medical formalities. It helped to have someone she knew with her so she didn't have to do it alone.

Lost in her own thoughts, she caught only snatches of Tyler's softly-spoken story.

Not good . . . miracle they both survived . . . the car was totaled . . .

Oh God. She squeezed her eyes shut. What if . . . he was already dead? No, surely somebody would have told them by now if that were the case.

More minutes crawled by. Mr. Bryant reached over and took her hand, smoothing his thumb over the back of it in a comforting gesture. She glimpsed the sparkling diamond and gold encircling her fourth finger and tears trickled down her face. Was it only just hours ago she'd become Ezra Bryant's fiancée? She couldn't do this. She couldn't. She wanted to bolt through those doors and run until she couldn't breathe. Run back in time to a place where none of this had ever happened. Maybe she'd wake up and find that it hadn't. . . .

Mr. Bryant squeezed her hand as if reading her thoughts, and she looked up at him, not caring a whit that he saw her crying. Moisture sparkled in his green eyes, so like his son's. "Hey," he said. "It's going to be okay. I know . . ." He swallowed hard. "My son picked a strong, courageous young woman. And you'll make it through this. I can promise you that. And whatever happens, know that I already consider you a daughter, and always will. Whatever happens." His voice broke and he bowed his head.

She blinked rapidly and clutched his hand in both of hers, resting her head on his shoulder.

A daughter. When had she last been a daughter?

You have always been My daughter, and I am holding you right now.

The words whispered through her heart, bringing with them a blanket of peace that settled around her.

Piper closed her eyes as happy memories of times spent with Ezra filled her mind. Some from more recent, and some from years ago. Paul and Ezra teasing her. Paul threatening to go after a schoolmate who'd made her cry and Ezra holding him back. Her sixteen-year-old-self curled up on the sofa between Paul and Ezra as they watched a movie at Paul's apartment.

Piper inhaled deeply and released it as Mr. Bryant started praying aloud.

Finally, a doctor entered the waiting area and glanced around the nearly empty room before coming towards them. Piper straightened, heart in her throat.

"Are you Ezra Bryant's family?" the doctor asked.

"We are." Mr. Bryant answered for them as he stood and pulled her to her feet before offering his hand to the doctor. "Tom Bryant, his father. This is Piper Redding, Ezra's fiancée, and Tyler Collens, a friend."

The doctor nodded and shook each of their hands. "Doctor Michaeles." He turned back to Mr. Bryant. "Your son is still unconscious, but currently stable."

A collective breath seemed to escape all
them and Piper's heart slowly slid back to where .
belonged.

"If you'll follow me," the man continued, "we can
further discuss his condition."

His condition. The words hit like a sledgehammer
and reality popped back in with startling clarity. Mr.
Bryant gripped her hand again, this time seemingly to
be comforted just as much to comfort, and the three
followed the doctor to a small private waiting room.
They each took a seat and Dr. Michaeles leaned
forward, resting his elbows on his knees and clasping
his hands. It would take a saw to cut the tension in the
room as the doctor gathered a breath before speaking.

"Ezra has suffered a severe traumatic brain injury,
in addition to three broken ribs on his left side from the
impact and some cuts and contusions from the shattered
glass, as I see this young lady has." He gestured to Piper
before continuing. "The ribs will heal in four to six
weeks, with no complications. They didn't puncture a
lung or cause any further internal damage, which is
lucky. Same with the cuts. They're only superficial and
will heal quickly.

"As for the head trauma, he hasn't roused or shown
any response to pain or stimuli yet. We did a CT scan,
which showed no fractures or bleeding in the brain,
which is a good thing. There is, however, some swelling
of the brain tissue, causing pressure inside the skull. We
inserted a probe into the skull to monitor the pressure,

and if it reaches a certain point, he may need surgery to relieve it to avoid causing any further brain damage. He's stable for now, though. As for prognosis, he could sleep for a few hours and wake up completely fine, or . . ." The doctor scrunched his mouth to the side as if he didn't like what he had to say. "Or he could potentially never wake up. It's too soon to know. I'm sorry to be so blunt, but I don't believe in false hope. I wish I could give you something more definite, but . . ." He spread his hands and shrugged his shoulders. "I've ordered an MRI, after which he will be moved to ICU where we'll monitor him for the next twenty-four to forty-eight hours and see what happens."

Dr. Michaeles was quiet for a few moments as he allowed them to process all he'd told them. Tyler hunched forward and fiddled with his hands. Mr. Bryant still held her hand and absently stroked it. Piper sat silently staring at a crack on the floor, watching as the tile seemed to spin in circles.

Never wake up . . .

Finally, the doctor cleared his throat and she jerked. "Do any of you have any questions?"

Mr. Bryant spoke first. "Can we see him?"

Dr. Michaeles nodded. "Of course. I'll have a nurse come for you as soon as he's settled in ICU. It's been proven to be beneficial to have those a patient loves around them even when unconscious. Just be prepared, he may look pretty rough to you."

Mr. Bryant nodded and Tyler asked a few more medically detailed questions she couldn't follow before the doctor stood. He sent a concerned glance her way as he did so. "Is there anything else I can do for you?"

Mr. Bryant looked at her as well and just shook his head. The doctor left. Ezra's father stood and pulled her into his arms in a futile attempt at comfort.

Piper felt empty—numb. She wasn't sure what she should feel if she could. *Never wake up.*

God, I need You.

Live Without You

17

Piper and the others followed the nurse into Ezra's room in the ICU. He checked the various monitors and displays by the bedside before stepping back and motioning them forward with an encouraging smile. With a gentle hand on her back, Mr. Bryant guided her towards the bedside while Tyler stood on the outskirts of the room to give them some space. She'd tried to prepare herself, but at the first sight of Ezra her lungs constricted and she felt the blood rush downward from her face.

He lay completely motionless on the bed except for the slow, steady rise and fall of his chest. His face was completely white beneath the angry-red cuts and scrapes. The left side of his face was bruised and swollen and more welts covered his lower arms and the backs of his hands. An IV protruded from one and an oxygen monitor was on his index finger. Oxygen prongs protruded from his nostrils, and the monitor the doctor had mentioned was attached to the top of his head.

If it weren't for the movement of his chest as he breathed, she'd think him dead.

Her heart seemed to miss a beat and she pressed a fist to her mouth and ran from the room before anyone could stop her. Leaning against the opposite wall, she slid to the floor, pressing her face to her knees. *God, I can't do this. Don't make me go through this. I can't,* she cried. He said He was holding her, but it felt far from it right now. All she had was faith, and that felt as thin as a thread, able to be snapped with the slightest pressure. More tears fell and she saw Ezra's blood-covered form on the ambulance gurney again. Then it was Paul, lying in the street in a pool of blood. Back and forth the two images rotated through her brain.

Suddenly, arms enfolded her, rocking her back and forth, shushing as a mother would her infant. And then the voice started speaking scripture softly into her ear.

"Fear not, for I have redeemed you. I have called you by name, you are Mine. When you pass through the waters I will be with you. When you walk through the fire you shall not be burned. For I am the Lord your God, your Savior. Fear not, I am with you . . ."

The rocking kept up until finally Piper pulled back. "How did you know?"

Miss Cecile smiled. "Tyler called me. I came as soon as I could." She wiped the tears from Piper's face with a tissue, careful to avoid the tender cuts and scrapes. More tears welled up in place of the ones she wiped away.

"I can't do this, Miss Cecile. I can't."

The nurse looked straight into Piper's eyes, firmness and confidence in the brown depths. "You can. And you will. You need to be strong for that man of yours, and the Lord says there ain't nothing you can't do with His help. He's got'cha, darlin'. Now you get back in there and let the boy know you're there for him. Got it?" Miss Cecile rose to her feet with surprising ease, considering her bulk, and tugged her up. Piper took a deep breath and looked at Miss Cecile one more time before stepping into the room. The woman gave a firm nod and Piper put one foot in front of the other.

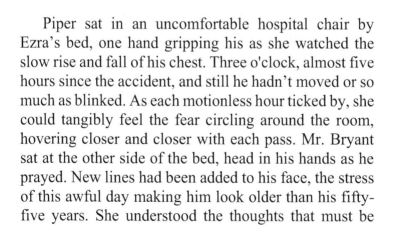

Piper sat in an uncomfortable hospital chair by Ezra's bed, one hand gripping his as she watched the slow rise and fall of his chest. Three o'clock, almost five hours since the accident, and still he hadn't moved or so much as blinked. As each motionless hour ticked by, she could tangibly feel the fear circling around the room, hovering closer and closer with each pass. Mr. Bryant sat at the other side of the bed, head in his hands as he prayed. New lines had been added to his face, the stress of this awful day making him look older than his fifty-five years. She understood the thoughts that must be running through his head. They'd both lost a loved one, and were now in keen danger of losing another.

Tyler had prowled around the room, seemingly unable to be still. He'd left a few minutes ago to get ready for work. Ezra should be getting ready for work now as well . . . The thought pierced. Piper shifted in her chair as the monitors beat their steady rhythm and rested her head on her arms, putting her own restlessness into prayers. For Ezra. For herself, for Mr. Bryant and their extended family. For Ezra's friends, Tyler. So many loved this man, and they were all hurting because he was hurting. She stroked his hand again and raised her head, speaking softly.

"You've got wake up, Ez. So many people love you. You can't leave yet . . . I need you. I . . ." Her voice broke. "I can't live without you." Tears fell again and she sniffed them back. She had to be strong. Pulling out the small card Miss Cecile had written on and slipped into her pocket, Piper read it again. "My grace is sufficient for you, for My strength is made perfect in weakness." Such simple words, but so hard to live by. She rested her head on her arms again and continued alternating praying and thinking as the long vigil grew longer.

"Piper. Piper."

Ezra was calling her. She had to wake up. Her head shot up and she blearily rubbed her eyes and looked to Ezra. But he was completely still, yet sleeping the sleep of the comatose. A hand was on her shoulder as her name was called again. She turned to find Mr. Bryant behind her.

"Piper, I was going to run to my house real quick and grab some things. Do you want me to take you home?"

"No!" Panic lit her tone. "Please don't make me leave, Mr. Bryant. Let me stay," she pleaded.

His gaze softened and he wrapped an arm around her trembling shoulders. She was strangely and suddenly cold. "Of course I won't make you go. I just thought you'd want to be home. I'll be back in about a half hour, all right?" She nodded and he patted her shoulder. "Oh, and it's Tom, okay?" he added, smiling softly. She gave a weak smile back and nodded again.

He turned to leave, the stoop of his shoulders attesting to his weariness. A nurse came in just as he left and checked the various monitors and displays, clicking keys and changing the IV. She wished it was Miss Cecile, but she didn't work in the ICU. The nurse finally finished her work and wrote a few notes for the doctor on the clipboard at the foot of the bed before turning to Piper with a kindly smile.

"Anything I can get you, hon?"

She thought for a moment, absentmindedly rubbing her arms. "A blanket would be nice, thank you."

"Of course." The nurse nodded and left, coming back with a blanket a short time later.

Piper tucked the blanket around herself and looked at Ezra. The swelling on the left side of his face had only gotten worse as the day went on. The doctor had said his face likely slammed into the doorframe at the impact, causing the bruising. She ran a finger lightly over the swelling. Her face didn't look the greatest either with the cuts that still stung, but it was nothing in comparison to this. Her heart clenched. She couldn't imagine the kind of pain he would be in if . . . when he awoke.

She sat there for a few more minutes until an idea came to her. Pulling out her phone, she scrolled to a Bible app. She opened it to the book of John, and, phone in one hand, Ezra's hand in the other, she started reading aloud.

"In the beginning was the Word, and the Word was with God, and the Word was God . . ."

Piper continued reading, barely looking up when Mr. Bryant—Tom—came in. She made it until the fourteenth chapter and her voice choked as she read the verses about the many mansions in the Father's house. She squeezed her eyes shut and quelled the rising emotion. She couldn't think about that. She couldn't.

Tom cleared his throat and she looked up. He held out a hand. Piper gave him her phone and he continued reading where she left off. He continued on through the betrayal and arrest, Jesus's imprisonment and death. Then the resurrection and the empty tomb. Hope swirled in Piper's heart. Ezra wasn't dead, but she hoped the morning would bring an empty hospital bed. Tom's deep voice and the words of Jesus soothed her, and she slept dreamlessly, her head pillowed on the scratchy hospital sheets as she held Ezra's hand.

Live Without You

18

Piper watched as the sun was just starting to sparkle through the second story windows of the hospital. Because of ICU policy, she'd had to go home for the night, but was back bright and early. Tom sat in the bedside chair now, head pillowed on his hands, legs crossed as he slept. He'd changed from the business attire he'd arrived at the hospital in yesterday to faded jeans and a rumpled green button-down.

She looked to the hospital bed. Nothing seemed to have changed. The blanket smoothed across Ezra's chest still rose and fell in the gentle rhythm of his breathing. His eyes were still closed, the cuts scabbed over on his face, the bruising turned yellowish-purple. The monitors still beeped softly, the IV still dripped clear fluids into his arm. Everything was as it had been for the last who-knew-how-many hours. Piper sighed wearily and rubbed her eyes as the door opened and the doctor stepped quietly in. He smiled and gave her a softly spoken "good morning" before turning towards his patient. He check Ezra's eyes and vitals, examined the injuries on his face and gently probed his ribs, watching all the while for any response from Ezra. He then turned towards the computers and monitors and spent several minutes there.

In the meantime, Tom stirred in his chair. His eyes popped open and shot to Ezra, then to the doctor, then to her before he slumped slightly in the chair. Piper stood and placed a hand on his shoulder and he reached up and gripped it as they waited.

Finally, the doctor turned towards them and sighed. "No change yet. His vitals are still steady and I'll order another CT scan a bit later to make sure all is still normal on the inside. But otherwise, he's just sleeping very deeply." He cleared his throat and examined his loafers before speaking again. "I want to prepare you, if he   does   wake up—"

"When." Tom's rumbling voice, still heavy with sleep, interrupted.

The doctor hesitated before nodding his concession. "—there still could be a severe amount of damage to deal with. He could have amnesia—temporary memory loss—or other brain damage. From the scans, I don't see any evidence of the latter as of now, but the former is a strong possibility. I just wanted you to be prepared.

Please rest assured we are doing everything medically possible for Ezra."

Tom slowly nodded and cleared his throat. "Thank you, Dr. Michaeles."

The man dipped his head and left, the door softly clicking shut behind him, sounding loud in the silence.

"If . . . amnesia . . . brain damage . . . if he wakes up."

The doctor's dire words swirled through her brain making her feel faint and numb at the same time. If the doctor wasn't hopeful . . . Shock and despair slowly spread through her body and limbs, weighing her down.

"Piper? Piper!" Alarm tinged Tom's voice as he stared at her. She stared unblinkingly back. "Sit down before you fall down." He hastily pushed her into the chair he vacated and leaned her forward, rubbing brisk circles on her back. Kneeling in front of her, he tipped her face so she had no choice but to look him in the face. "Piper, look at me. Take a deep breath. C'mon, take a deep breath."

She finally forced her leaden lungs to expand and the dizziness and black spots crowding her vision faded.

Tom nodded encouragingly. "Good girl. Another. Now listen to me, Piper." He waited until she met his eyes. They were more gray than green, as she'd noticed Ezra's were when he was upset. "You're okay, we're okay. God is right here, and He hasn't left, nor will He.

He promises He's here with us and for us. Okay?" She nodded. He was here. His grace was sufficient . . . She closed her eyes and took another deep breath and when she opened them, Ezra's father was still searching her face, making sure she was all right.

"Will . . . will you pray?" she asked.

The tension in his face softened. "Of course."

19

The seemingly endless agony of waiting continued. Friends, family, and even Ezra's co-workers visited briefly and offered prayers before leaving again. With the stream of visitors, it was clear Ezra was a popular guy. Piper was exhausted merely by having to smile and say thank-you repeatedly. No one mentioned Piper and Ezra's engagement, and she was almost glad for it.

The future felt too uncertain to even mention it.

In the afternoon, a small group comprised of a few church friends, Tyler, Cecile, and their pastor all gathered in a circle around Ezra's bed, praying, sometimes silently, sometimes aloud. A small gathering of believers interceding for one of their own in his time of need. Piper was moved to tears by the beauty of it.

She only wished it wasn't so desperately necessary.

A while later, the doctor came in.

"I have some not-so-great, but thankfully manageable news," he announced. Piper had to take a slow breath to steady her suddenly racing heart. "In the scan done this morning, it showed a bit of bleeding in Ezra's brain. That's not good, but, it was just a small amount, and I feel confident that it will stop and dry up on its own, no surgery necessary."

Piper exhaled and sat down by Ezra again. She took his hand, longing to feel his fingers tighten around hers, for his green eyes to open and for him to grin that grin she loved. *Ezra Christopher Bryant, you have to wake up. I can't lose you too. I can't lose you. I love you.* She brought his hand to her lips and kissed his fingers before resting it against her cheek. She fell asleep like that until Tom shook her shoulder and urged her to go home.

Feeling bone and soul weary with no fight left in her, she relented after making Tom promise to call her if anything changed.

He hugged her tightly and whispered into her hair. "I promise."

20

When Piper arrived at the hospital the next morning, nothing had changed. In fact, they seemed to have gotten worse. Ezra's face was paler, his breathing slower and labored. Tom was grayer and despair flickered in his eyes, though she noticed he made a conscious effort to hide it.

Four days.

Four long days, and still they paced and watched and waited as Ezra seemed to slip further and further away. After the doctor and nurses had left after one of their regular checks, Piper slid to her knees by the bedside and rested her head on the blanket. Tom had left to go home and sleep for a few hours, so she was alone in the room. Despair wore heavily on her heart, and she felt she didn't have the strength to fight it anymore. She poured her heart out before her heavenly Father and her anguish in salty tears.

"Oh God. I can't do this. I can't. I need him. Please don't take him from me. You can't take him from me. Help me. I am so, so tired." Shudders continued to wrack her body long after the tears had stopped.

Then a still, small voice spoke into her torrent of thoughts.

"Will you live without him if that is My will? Can I be enough for you?"

Piper stopped moving and breathing altogether for the space of a few moments. Would she? Could she? Her brain knew the right answer, but her heart didn't want to acquiesce. *Please don't ask that of me,* she begged.

"Will you give Me your all and allow Me to be your everything?" The voice demanded an answer, but was still gentle. He Himself had even given up His Loved One, His own Son. For her. Could she give Him her loved one and trust herself into His hands?

Answering that question felt like falling backward in a trust fall. She'd always hated trust falls. Could she do it now? God's arms were more trustworthy than anyone else's. Logic warred with her heart seemingly indefinitely.

Piper took a deep breath and let it out slowly, expelling her doubts, her fears. "Help me surrender, Lord. I surrender. Take my all for I am Yours."

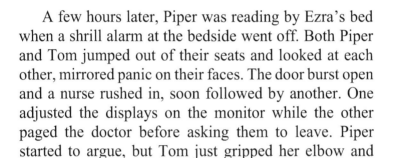

A few hours later, Piper was reading by Ezra's bed when a shrill alarm at the bedside went off. Both Piper and Tom jumped out of their seats and looked at each other, mirrored panic on their faces. The door burst open and a nurse rushed in, soon followed by another. One adjusted the displays on the monitor while the other paged the doctor before asking them to leave. Piper started to argue, but Tom just gripped her elbow and gently led her out the door. They found seats in a small, nearly empty waiting area. Instead of sitting, Tom paced the room like a caged animal, tension filling the air. Piper watched him, her thoughts running faster than his footsteps.

One, two, three, four, turn.

One, two, three, back.

And repeat. Finally, he took a deep breath and sat in the chair next to her, taking her hands and bowing his head. He started to pray. Piper wanted to join in, but the words stuck in her throat. Her heart cried out instead, internally voicing her greatest fears. Soon a blanket of peace covered her, assuring her she was still in God's arms. As was Ezra. And Tom.

What seemed like hours later, the doctor finally stepped into the room and strode over to them. "He's fine," he reassured as he took a seat next to them. "Although it may not have seemed like it, this was a good thing. Ezra's heart rate accelerated, causing the alarm to go off. The likely cause was excitement or agitation. Could have been a reaction to pain—we haven't been giving him a ton of pain meds as I didn't want to add to his non-reactionary state—or to your voices, perhaps. Either way, this was a good thing," he reiterated. "It means he could possibly be on his way to consciousness. We'll know more in the next couple of hours, hopefully."

Piper exhaled, seemingly for the first time in days. She felt like she'd been on the edge of her seat, holding her breath for a bit of hope. And here it was. She felt lighter as she thanked the doctor. She turned to Tom with the first real—though shaky—smile in what felt like a long time. He clutched her tightly, whispering into her hair. "It's going to be okay. It's going to be okay."

"It's going to be okay."

21

He was swimming. In a black sea of nothingness. He couldn't see anything, feel anything. He heard faint voices, but couldn't make them out. He felt detached from reality, living in a foreign universe in outer space. He thought about Piper. Was she okay? Something had happened, he knew, but he didn't know what. Everything was foggy, shrouded by an opaque mist. Was she worried about him? Where was he, anyway? If he knew, he'd be able to find a way back to her.

Back to light. Reality.

Life.

Despair crashed over him. He was failing again now. He didn't know how, but he was. He'd always been a failure. He didn't save his mom . . . was this his punishment? That didn't fit with the picture of a loving

God, but . . . Was this hell? He thought hell would be hot, fiery. But this was dark, and cold, actually. . . .

A gentle voice floated through his head as he drifted off again. *"I've prepared a beautiful place for you. But it is not yet your time. You have done well, My faithful servant, and I have much more for you to do."*

"But Lord," he protested, feeling his utter unworthiness. *"I can't. I've failed You again and again. You can't possibly use me."*

"In your unworthiness is where you have worth. My power works through you, My strength is made perfect in your weakness. You have given Me your heart and your best; that is all I ask."

The words washed through his brain, rolling over and over and echoing off the corridors of his mind like waves on the shore. He wanted to hold onto this beautiful moment, those beautiful words, but he felt himself drifting again, like an unmoored boat.

The morning ticked by as slowly as usual. Tyler dropped by before work. A new kind of impatience welled up in Piper. She missed Ezra. She'd fully committed him to God now, whether he lived or died, so she tried to stem her impatience. Piper and Tom had just finished what had become their daily prayer time around Ezra's bed when something caught Piper's eye.

His hand. It moved. Barely, but it was more than before. She glanced at Tom and saw he had seen it too. Piper reached for Ezra's hand, taking it gently in her own.

"Ezra?" she called. "Ez, it's me, Piper." No response . . . but then his dark eyelashes fluttered against the contrast of his pale face before slowly opening. He groaned as if pulling himself from a deep well, startling both her and Tom. Then he blinked up at her before his eyes shifted to Tom's face hovering on the other side of the bed.

Then he smiled.

"Hey," he said before his eyes flickered shut again. Piper wanted to laugh with joy, but it came out more as a sob. She noted tears in Tom's eyes as well.

Ezra's eyes opened again and this time his gaze was steadier. "Why's everyone crying? What happened anyway?" He shifted slightly, then moaned and clutched a hand to his chest, hesitantly sucking in a breath. Tom moved to press the nurse call button.

"Hey, shh . . ." Piper laid her palm on his chest to make him hold still. "You were in a car accident. You broke a few ribs and have been in a coma for five days."

A frown flitted across his face. "Oh." He looked at her again. "Why are you crying?" His tone was gently reproachful and he reached up a hand towards her face, but it was shaky. She grabbed it and clasped it against her cheek instead.

He was back. And he remembered. More tears fell as she silently praised God.

"I'm happy, Ez. I was so scared . . ." Her voice hitched. "I love you, Ezra Bryant." She pressed a kiss to his forehead and pulled away, running her fingers gently over the neatly healing cuts on his face.

He grinned—oh, that grin. Weak, but the same grin nonetheless. "Hey, if I get this kind of treatment, it might be in my best interest to be in a coma again."

"Ezra!" She gave him a mock glare, but it failed. She couldn't even pretend to be mad at him right now. "Don't you dare do that again, do you hear me?"

Smiling gently, he minutely tightened his grip on her fingers. "Yes, ma'am," he whispered.

"Well, Ezra, you gave your family and friends quite a scare there. How are you feeling?" The doctor gently thumbed open Ezra's eyelids and examined his eyes with a penlight. They watered as the bright light sent a sharp pain ricocheting through his skull.

"Not to sound cliché, but kinda like I got hit by a Mack truck."

The man chuckled and pocketed the penlight. "Well, almost. It was a Dodge, I believe. Feel like you can sit up a bit?" Ezra nodded and the doctor pressed a button, the bed tilting to bring him semi-upright. Ezra blinked and clenched his teeth against the massive headrush and pain in his ribs, barely suppressing a groan. Little dwarves with not-so-little jackhammers were pounding away inside his skull and every breath sent agony through his rib cage.

"Now how's the pain?" the doctor asked.

"Fine," Ezra gritted out, very aware of his dad and Piper looking concernedly on in the background. Dr. Michaeles raised his brows and made a note on his clipboard. "Right. We'll get some pain meds running through your veins again and you'll feel much better."

Ezra was too tired to respond with a sarcastic remark. After poking and prodding Ezra's ribs and the bruises on his face, the doctor left with the admonition to take it easy. As if Ezra had the strength or willpower to do anything but. He said they would take one more brain scan to make sure all was as it should be and keep him for observation for another day or two. Then he could go home.

Within minutes of the nurse inserting the medication into his IV, Ezra felt like he was floating again and the pain was blissfully absent. Sweet relief. Then his dad and Piper were at his side again, his dad's arm around her shoulders. Ezra smiled tiredly and reached up. His fiancée took his hand. "Take care of my girl, Dad," he said before his eyes slid shut of their own volition.

"Oh, I have been," Tom said, a smile in his voice.

---◆---

Tom's arm tightened around her shoulders and she smiled, her hand still holding Ezra's. His girl. She was God's girl, then Ezra's. And she felt blissfully content. All was right with the world. *Thank you for answering our prayers, Father,* she prayed silently.

She and Tom stood at the bedside a moment more. Ezra was battered and bruised, and oh so weak, but he was here. Suddenly his eyes fluttered open again and fixated on her face. "Piper, please marry me." His voice was already groggy and slightly slurred.

A jolt of alarm shot through her. Had he forgotten? She gave a nervous giggle. "Of course. But we did this once already. Did you forget?"

He smiled and closed his eyes again. "Nope. Just checking." He brought her hand to his lips and kissed it, clinging tightly to it with both hands as his breathing steadied in sleep.

Piper fought tears again. She knew this man loved her with all his heart. What more could she ask for? Tom brought her a chair so she didn't have to remove her hand. Soon, she fell asleep too, head pillowed on the edge of the bed, her hand encased in her beloved's as she dreamed of the future.

22

The next forty-eight hours passed quickly, to Ezra's relief. He hated being sick and he hated being the center of attention. His dad insisted Ezra stay with him until he was fully healed, and he agreed. He knew head injuries weren't to be messed with. Not to mention the mere act of breathing still felt like being stabbed with tiny swords.

Finally after settling in at his dad's, he lay sprawled on the couch with his eyes closed, resting. He'd refused the bed. Dumb move, now that he thought about it. He couldn't remember the last time he'd had a headache like this one. He drifted to sleep, the peace and quiet lacking the beeping and whooshing of hospital machines lulling him into oblivion.

His mother stood over him, smiling down at him. She looked healthy, whole, and the happiest he'd ever seen her. She stroked the hair back from his forehead with a gentle touch that spoke of love.

"Mom!" he said in surprise, sitting up.

"Ezra, my son," she cupped his chin in her hand, tilting his face up to meet her eyes that crinkled at the corners. "Thank you," she said, a choke in her voice. "You always took such good care of me. I love you so much, my Ezzie."

His throat convulsed as he tried to swallow the lump that had risen in it. "I love you too, Mom."

She stared into his eyes for a moment more, love reflecting back at him from her brilliant blue ones. Like sapphires, his father had always said. "I know," she whispered. Then she pressed a kiss to his forehead.

Ezra's eyes flew open, his chest heaving, causing shards of pain to spread through his torso. Piper stood above him, smiling at him.

"Piper," he said, voice still ragged with the emotion of his dream. "She was there. Here. She—" His voice cracked. "She thanked me."

Piper knelt by the couch, confusion wrinkling her brow. "Who did, Ez?"

"My mom." He could feel moisture sliding down his face but he didn't care. She'd thanked him. It was okay. He'd given his best and that was all she—and his heavenly Father—had ever wanted. Somehow it had taken this to truly cement it in his head. He told the dream to Piper.

"Aw, Ez . . ." Piper smoothed the hair back from his forehead with a soft hand, much the way his mother had done in his dream and when he was a little boy. Understanding softened her features and unshed tears sparkled in her eyes. More tears fell from his own and he pulled her into his arms, ignoring the pain and burying his face in her neck, overwhelmed with the emotion.

It was okay. No matter what anyone might try to tell him, he was not a failure. It was okay. . . .

Piper sat with Ezra's arms around her. The enormity of his dream wasn't lost on her. She hugged him tighter and he flinched. She immediately pulled back, remembering his healing ribs.

"Oh! Sorry!"

He shook his head, lightly wincing as he rubbed gentle fingers over his side. "I'll be so happy when these are healed." He paused, staring at the carpet before looking at her, emotion darkening his eyes again. "We're so blessed."

She nodded, too choked to make a response.

"I love you, Piper."

"I love you too, Ezra." She smiled up into his handsome face made no less so by the fading marks and bruises. "Can we pray together?" she asked.

He smiled. "I'd like that." They clasped each other's hands and bowed their heads, praising their heavenly Father for His grace and love, basking in the assurance that come what may, they would never have to live without Him.

epilogue

The late afternoon sunlight flickered through the trees, shedding golden light on the group below. A brisk early November breeze blew lightly, chilling the air and softly rustling the crisp leaves of autumn.

Adorned in a simple cream dress with a tulle skirt and a bouquet of sage and earthy-toned flowers and succulents in her hand, the bride was escorted to the greenery-bedecked arbor by her future father-in-law. After dropping a kiss on her forehead, he placed her hands in his son's, who was standing under the arbor and manfully struggling to hold back tears. Dressed in a gray waistcoat replete with a sage-colored pocket square and tie, the groom took his bride's hands.

She met his eyes through the sheer veil, complete love and trust shining from them. Likewise, promise shone from his. The minister led the couple through their vows as they pledged themselves to the other, till death parted them. To some, those words were a trite repetition of tradition. But to the couple, it held an even greater and deeper meaning than for most, for they both knew death on an intimate level. Both knew that God had drawn them together, mended their broken pieces, and they trusted their future to Him, whatever it contained.

"I now pronounce you husband and wife. Therefore, what God has joined together, let no man separate." The minister intoned before turning to the groom. "Son, and now for the first time, you may kiss your bride."

The groom grinned and gently lifted the veil over the bride's head, her burnished brown hair and the lace tiara tucked into it glinting in the sunlight. Cupping her face with both hands, he captured her lips in a sweet kiss. The crowd clapped wildly and there were few dry eyes.

"Till death do us part," he whispered as he pulled away.

"Till death do us part," she repeated, smiling up at him.

Then, tucking her hand in the crook of his arm, the groom escorted his wife back down the aisle, both of them with smiles fit to break their faces.

Through much pain and heartache, God's love triumphs over fear, and His grace over guilt.

Acknowledgements

I never set out to write a novella, no less publish it, but here I am! Yet *Live Without You* would still be sitting in a basement in a tattered notebook, buried in dust and who-knows-what-else if it wasn't for the help of some pretty amazing people.

The first thank you goes to my little sis, Isabella. Thanks for listening to me think out loud (aka, ramble endlessly) into the wee hours of the morning, brainstorming with me in the tall grass behind the pond, and most importantly, thank you for the exploding Christmas lightbulb backstory. That was awesome. Love you, Jones!

A huge thank you to Victoria Lynn for paving the publishing way for me, for the beautiful formatting job, all the advice, encouragement and publishing help, and most importantly, for being my big sis! I love you!

To my family: thank you for supporting me in all of my dreams. To my older brothers: thanks for all the practice in sarcasm and banter. I owe it all to you. ;) And to my little brothers, thanks for making this writer's heart happy by begging me to write faster and to let you read the first draft. To Rebecca, my most wonderful sister-in-law: thanks for catching all those final draft errors! It would have been pretty embarrassing for me if you hadn't. ;)

Another big thank you goes to Allison Tebo, Mary H. and Micaiah K. Alli, thanks for being my honorary big sis and quite possibly my biggest supporter! I wuv you! Mary, thank you for always being there for me in all things, and for believing in me and my dreams. What would I do without my practical Mary to steady my flighty soul? Micaiah . . . darling, thank you for being you! Thank you for fangirling over my story, for all the laughter shared, and most of all, for being my 'bosom friend!' I hope to one day soon see one of YOUR stories published! Love ya, my girlie!

Thank you to my alpha readers, Faith Potts, Hosanna K., Jesseca Wheaton, Maddy C., and Micaiah K.! Your fabulous feedback gave me the confidence I needed to push me to publishing, and gave LWY a hefty dose of much-needed polish!

To my beta readers, Addy S., Chloe W., Ivie Brooks, J.D. Sutter, Kate Willis, Lilian S., Lisa E., Mikayla H., and Rebecca Grzybowski: Y'all were so incredibly encouraging in your feedback and did an awesome job cleaning up my messy draft. I can't thank you enough for all the hard work and time you put into making *Live Without You* the best it could be!

To my proofreader, Bridget Marshall: Wow, girl! What would I have done without you? You did such a thorough job, and if there are any errors left, it's entirely my fault. Thank you!

A special thank you goes to author and ER nurse, Jordyn Redwood for answering my questions about gunshot wounds and helping me come up with a plausible and realistic scenario.

A shout-out to the Goodreads community is most necessary. You know who you are! I feel so blessed to be part of such a supportive group of people like y'all!

Another shout-out to the Christian Writers' Encouragement Hangouts Group and the Chatterbox NaNo cabin: what an amazing group of ladies you all are! Thank you for the support, encouragement, prayers, and all those sprints in April and July 2018 NaNos that helped me push through and finish the first and second drafts of LWY! I'm not sure I would have finished if it wasn't for y'all!

And finally, most important of all, thank you to my Jesus. For putting this story in my head and guiding me as I wrote it. For rescuing me out of my darkness and bringing me into Your marvelous light. And for silencing the voices in my head and singing Your love over me. All glory and honor to you, precious Savior.

Sarah Grace Gray

Author bio

Sarah Grace Grzy is a voracious reader, and if it weren't for this crazy thing called 'Life,' she'd be tempted to spend all her days in front of a wood stove, book in one hand, coffee mug in the other. A lover of learning, she finds enjoyment in many things and has more hobbies than she knows what to do with. Sarah Grace is a freelance web and graphic designer, and when not working, spending time with her ever-growing family, or reading, she can be found painting, playing the piano, or fangirling with her sisters and friends. Sarah Grace inhabits the State of Great Lakes, and wouldn't want to live anywhere else—unless it meant she could have a baby penguin, in which case, she'd gladly move to the South Pole.

Estetico designs

web and graphic design

WEB DESIGN

BLOG REDESIGN

LOGOS

BOOK COVERS · EBOOK + PAPERBACK

PROMOTIONAL GRAPHICS

+ MORE!

WWW.ESTETICODESIGNS.COM

ESTETICODESIGNS@GMAIL.COM

VICTORIA LYNN DESIGNS

AFFORDABLE INDIE PUBLISHING SERVICES

Professional ~ Quick ~ Affordable

Put your best foot forward into the publishing world

COVER DESIGN E-BOOK AND PAPERBACK
INTERIOR PAPERBACK FORMATTING
KINDLE FORMATTING
BLOG TOUR SERVICES
BETA READING SERVICES
GRAPHIC DESIGN

CONTACT

WWW.VICTORIALYNNDESIGNS.COM

rufflesandgrace@gmail.com

Made in the USA
Middletown, DE
31 January 2020